# They Were Dreamers and Doers

# They Were Dreamers and Doers

## Pioneer Faith in Action

KATHLEEN PITNEY BOX

RESOURCE *Publications* · Eugene, Oregon

THEY WERE DREAMERS AND DOERS
Pioneer Faith in Action

Resource Publications
An Imprint of Wipf and Stock Publishers
199 W. 8th Ave., Suite 3
Eugene, OR 97401

www.wipfandstock.com

PAPERBACK ISBN: 978-1-6667-6052-1
HARDCOVER ISBN: 978-1-6667-6053-8
EBOOK ISBN: 978-1-6667-6054-5

12/08/22

I dedicate this book to my 97-year-old mother, Barbara McFadden Pitney, who has lived through such changing times and shared so much of her own family history with me. Her family also crossed the plains and homesteaded in Oregon. She has patiently accompanied me as I've researched, traveled, and written only about Dad's family for the last ten years. Thank you for your support, Mom.

# Contents

You are about to read historic adventures accounted from my great-great grandfather's handwritten memoirs. He lived such an extraordinary life that it's provided two books of inspiration and historical enterprises with some interpretation from me. I have only imagined some details, procedures, and conversations to help explain some hows and whys of what he did. With much help, I've tried to stay true to the times, names, and locations. However, this is still called historical fiction. And of course, as so often is true, behind every great man was a strong, faithful wife supporting his many accomplishments. In James Bushnell's case, it took two strong women!

# Prologue

"Now once we get inside this special room, kids, I want you all to hold Grammy's hands or your parents' hands. These Bibles are terribly old, and we must be very, very careful."

Faith, Joya, and Marcus followed Mr. Steve, the librarian, toward a brown wooden door that he opened with a very old-looking key. Eight-year-old Marcus noticed that Mr. Steve had lots of keys and was curious about the man. Mr. Steve must be especially important. When Mr. Steve entered first into the narrow room, then Marcus knew he was an important man. Their grandmother was close behind and, once inside, reached out her hands to them. Faith and Marcus, the oldest two, obediently took a hand. Joya and the parents followed behind.

Grammy Kathy explained, "Mr. Steve will lay some of the special old Bibles down here on this low table for us to look at. Then we will let him turn the pages because they are so delicate and could easily tear. Some are many hundreds of years old and need to be protected. They all come from between the 14th and the 18th centuries. Faith, do you know how long a century is?"

Nine-year-old Faith scrunched her nose doubtfully, but replied, "Maybe a hundred years?"

Mr. Steve was putting on white cotton gloves before showing them a large black leather Bible from England.

"You're right, Faith!" Mr. Steve proclaimed. "So, this is the oldest Bible in the school's collection, a Wycliffe Bible. Many of these first Bibles were burned and were dangerous for people to read. And over here, we have a first edition Geneva Bible. This is a particularly important Bible because it was a first translation of the Bible into English. This type would have been used by William Shakespeare and John Bunyan. You may have heard of them. John Bunyan wrote Pilgrim's Progress."

Faith enthusiastically declared, "We've read *Little Pilgrims Progress* before. Or, really, our mom read it to us. There were lots of scary parts, but some happy parts, too. I think I was only seven then and I got scared really easy. I still get nightmares sometimes and my dad has to come into my room and sleep with me. I don't get them as much as I used to, though."

Grammy said, "Faith, look at this pretty page." She figured it was time to distract Faith from her many stories about nightmares. That little girl loved to talk!

The three curious grandchildren looked at the colored drawings of vines and flowers that were on the first page of the old black Bible Mr. Steve showed them. As he carefully turned the pages, he let Grammy look for some of her favorite verses. She read: "For by grace are ye saved through faith, and that not of yourselves: it is the gift of God, not of works, lest any man should boast himself. Ephesians 2:8–9."

After listening quietly, Marcus asked, "Grammy, does that Bible have the verse about the shepherd and his table with enemies?"

Grammy grinned. "It sure does! Every Bible, whether it's old or new, should have the same verses inside. Let's see. I think it's Psalm 23 you mean. Does that sound right to you, Marcus?"

"I think so," the little boy said, nodding his light brown-haired head.

"Well, here it is—Psalm 23, verse 1. 'The Lord is my Shepherd' and in verse 5, it says 'Thou dost prepare a table before me in the sight of my adversaries.' It sounds a little different from the way we say it, doesn't it, Marcus? This is in an old language that we've changed over many years."

"Yeah, that's it because I remember it says something about presents with his enemies."

That caused a lot of laughter all around the little boy. Marcus' dad came to his rescue and slowly explained, "The Bible was saying 'presence'—like who's there with you. In your presence. Not the gift kind of presents."

Marcus replied by turning and questioning his grandmother, "And does it talk about streams and grassy fields that sheep like, too?"

Grammy replied, "Well, yes it does."

Joya, the quieter of the three, said "Grammy, I like the gold letters and those colored flowers." She didn't say that she thought everything else in black-and-white was kind of boring. She could tell that her grandmother and her parents thought the pages were something special, so she just quietly looked around her.

Mr. Steve showed the children and their parents more old Bibles and books. Although the kids did like the Bibles in general, after a few more very plain old books, they were done. They tried to wait patiently, but finally Joya said, "Are there any kids' books in here?"

Her mother groaned, "Joya! This is not a place for kids' books. Haven't you been listening?"

Grammy just smiled and said, "Sorry, Joya, but this is a special room, just for old books and Bibles."

Grammy turned from her grandchildren and thanked Steve. Faith, Marcus, and Joya knew he had taken special time with them because somehow these old Bibles were important to their family. That made Faith wonder again, "How did we get related to these old Bibles, Grammy?"

"This room is named the Sarah Bushnell Rare Bible Collection. See the sign here by the door? That same Sarah was married to my great-great grandfather, James Bushnell. They gave money to their good friend, Mr. Sanderson, to go across the Atlantic Ocean to Europe and buy all these Bibles and books for this university. That was many, many years ago. The Bibles and books were a special gift from our long-ago relatives, and their story is special to our family and to me — and I wanted to share it with you kids and your parents. I am so glad you came with me!

"Now, who wants to go get some ice cream?"

# CHAPTER ONE

TWENTY-TWO-YEAR-OLD ELISABETH HAD JUST endured a very difficult 20-month separation and finally had her family back together. It had been 20 long and challenging months since her husband, James, left them on their farm in Adair County, Missouri, to strike his riches in the California gold fields. Left behind for nearly two years with their baby boy, she'd been forced to manage their farm and then cross over the country on the Oregon Trail.

Oh, how long ago it seemed since she'd left the comforts of her parents' lovely, well-tended home. Coming from a Virginia plantation, she had rarely done a speck of outdoor work, and even had plenty of help with indoor chores back then. That she had maintained their 80-acre farm and home for the whole duration of James' absence was astonishing. With plenty of help from James' brothers, and some from her mother-in-law and two sisters-in-law, Elisabeth did the best she could. Still, even with their help, it had been such a terribly unproductive year. All the neighboring farmers in the county were badly hurt, too—first by a cold, late spring, then a short summer season which was followed by an early harsh winter. It hit them hard. With that string of severe weather, little of her grueling work had paid off. She had been terribly discouraged.

Early next winter of 1853, some of the Bushnell family started to discuss giving up farming in Missouri (or "Misery," as some called it) and heading out west instead. The free land the government was promising in the mild and fertile Willamette Valley was awfully appealing. Plus, the Bushnell family could search for their two missing brothers: her James, and the older one, William. William had left for the gold fields a year before James. And, as with James, no word from William had ever reached the family back home in Missouri.

Elisabeth had been very uncertain about what she should do if the other Bushnells moved out west. In desperation, she wrote James another of her many letters. In this one she described his brother Jason and Mother Bushnell's persuasiveness, and her likely decision to sell the farm and head out west with them. As Mr. Baker, the Kirksville postmaster, had advised, she sent this last letter off to Oregon City because it had the most established post office of all the western settlements. It would be the most likely place James would look. So, off her letter went to Oregon City.

Still no word from James. What should she do? She was agonizing all alone over these hard decisions to make. Eventually, she gave in to her brother-in-law Jason's reasoning: they would be smart to give up on these farms and head out west for the free farmland in the mild Oregon climate.

Once the decision was made, everything happened quickly. Along with three other Bushnell families, she also sold her farm. She and little two-year-old Charles Alva joined Mother Bushnell; her brothers-in-law Jason, Corydon, and Edward; and her sisters-in-law Helen and Martha in getting ready to move. They all bought wagons, oxen, and supplies, and packed up their families. Mother Bushnell had the toughest time because she had ac-cumulated the most personal possessions after raising a large family in a comfortable home for many years. Elisabeth had teared up, watching her mother-in-law decide what to pack and what to leave behind—things she would likely never see again. But Mother Bushnell had an adventurous spirit and wasn't as bothered by the process as Elisabeth was! The hardest for both women was the painful moment when Elisabeth and the others watched Mother say goodbye to her remaining son George, his new wife Nancy and their six children, Mother's beloved grandchildren. This oldest brother hadn't been caught up in the lure of free land or gold as his younger brothers had.

Their westward journey was fairly smooth, but it turned hazardous when the Bushnells and others made the unfortunate decision to leave the much larger group and turn south at Fort Hall, following a new, more direct route to the middle Willamette Valley. That's where they aimed to settle and, hopefully, find James, so it made sense to the Bushnell family to head that way. Led by an inexperienced guide (they would learn later), they departed from the main trail and took a southern shortcut, along with 150 other wagons.

Their wagon train became lost for some time in the vast, arid deserts of eastern Oregon. Struggling along for weeks and nearly starving to death, they were finally rescued by some Willamette Valley settlers almost a month later. Once the word went out about the lost wagon train, a group of con-cerned settlers rode into the hills looking for them. That was how Elisabeth and her son ended up with the generous Briggs family. She had caught the attention of Isaac Briggs, who had organized and helped execute their big rescue. Her plight, lost and on her own with a toddler and no husband, touched his heart and they were offered a room in their home for as long as she needed it.

It was at the Briggs' home where James finally found her and little Charles. Elisabeth and James had independently survived journeys that many others did not. Despite the safe and happy reunion, their long separation had been quite traumatic for Elisabeth.

# CHAPTER TWO

**OCTOBER 1853**

BRUSHING THE DUST AND crumbs of chicken feed off her pale blue apron, Elisabeth also gave her head a shake to clear it. It was remarkable! After weeks of searching, James, her long-lost husband, had finally found them here in the tiny town of Springfield, Oregon. Here he was happily watching their two-and-a-half-year-old son climb up and down the wide, front steps where his parents sat. She was still mentally grappling with the fact that an untidy, rough-looking, bearded James had just walked up to the Briggs' residence a few minutes before, after his nearly two-year absence. Seeing his familiar frame–short but sturdy—and hearing his deep voice again had been quite a shock, but also delightful. After all this time apart, he'd found her, and she'd been a little embarrassed to be found in the chicken roost scolding the hens!

She had quickly put her egg basket down, and their initial embrace had been long and warm, but gentle. Surprisingly, she'd suddenly felt shy. Elisabeth pulled away first and began introducing, or reintroducing, James to little Charles. "Charles Alva, this is your daddy who we have been trying to find. And look—he found us!"

She watched James silently approach the lad, squat down to the little one's eye level and start to get acquainted with his son. The fatherly affection in his voice and the warmth he showed Charles stirred up a joy deep within Elisabeth. Her son finally had two parents again, and she had a husband!

At this point she realized her hosts were probably waiting for their breakfast eggs. She'd gathered just five warm, brown eggs before James walked up, but that was going to have to do for now. She gently picked up the basket from the step.

"James, the Briggs family needs to know you're here! I've got to go inside and tell them. Can you please stay with Charles while I go in and break the news?"

She stood up briskly and was up two steps before she turned back and smiled broadly at him, "It's just too good to be true. It's really you at last!"

"Yep, you can tell them it's really me, James Addison Bushnell, your long overdue husband," he said grinning up at her.

## TWO DAYS LATER

James firmly held the reins as he turned the pair of sorrel mares off the rough path they'd been trodding, and led them into the open field. After two hectic days, he and Elisabeth were finally alone together except for the sleeping Charles. They had borrowed the Briggs' wagon and were on their way to find his mother and brothers. He hoped it wasn't going to be too hard to find their new claims. Following the general directions Elisabeth had gathered from the Briggs, and a bit more she'd learned from Jason before he left, James sure hoped they were heading the right way. They'd left the golden hills of Springfield and were going towards the flat land to the west.

He and Elisabeth both tried to cover their disappointment when they learned that much of this open land had already been claimed. With few markings, and most of them rough and homemade, it was hard to know where one claim ended, and another began. So, they had asked everyone they met along their way about the land claims. They also asked if anyone had seen which direction the wagon of Bushnells had gone. Not many, but a few folks said they'd seen a group fitting the description James gave. Those few tried to be helpful but could only give James very limited directions. So, as James took to the open field, he could only hope for the best.

Bouncing along through the rough, swishing long grass seated next to her husband, Elisabeth was experiencing a topsy-turvy mixture of her own feelings. On one hand, she was grateful that her family was at last back together again. And, of course, she was also thankful that James was safe. He was healthy. His hands felt familiar and comforting when he touched her. The warmth in his eyes and voice was evidence of his love for her and for Charles. He was being truly kind and considerate; actually, more polite than she was used to.

Too soon, though, her initial gratefulness and joy had become muddied like the crude path the horses were following. That initial happiness now felt much less definite and smooth. She'd felt her first irritation surprisingly fast upon James' arrival and before she was ready to talk about it. It had hit her within the first day James arrived at the Briggs'. She had resented that James went off with the other men, right after the celebratory supper that Betsy Briggs and her daughter-in-law had prepared. First off, James had heartily entertained the Briggs and Elliott families around the table. He claimed he had enough stories about his adventures traveling the continent back and forth three times to fill a book! To his credit, he only told a few at that first meal.

Then, she'd patiently listened to him ask lots of questions of the elder Briggs, Isaac. James voiced his admiration repeatedly while listening to the Briggs men's inventiveness, their demanding work digging a mill race, and their final success at their sawmill. Elias Briggs, the son, had plenty to say as he began describing the luscious but undeveloped land which they found upon their arrival four years earlier. Next, Elisabeth watched as James charmed these men with his cheerful optimism and eagerness to learn. And so it was that soon after eating, all the men left to show the newcomer around. James had actually said he assumed that she and the other ladies "had womanly things to do." Again, too soon, she was left with busy little Charles Alva and the Briggs women

While brusquely sweeping the kitchen crumbs out the door, she saw and heard the menfolk as they headed over north of the big house. She knew that was where they'd show off the mill race and their mill. Elias and Isaac had a right to be proud of their small community store, mill and the new blacksmith shop. The Briggs certainly had one of the nicest houses around here, too. It was then it struck her that James was following the Briggs men around like a bouncing puppy, waging its tail and wanting to please. She couldn't help but hear his loud exclamations across the yard, and it was easy enough to tell he was very impressed.

Yes, in less than a day, James' focus had shifted from being with his own family, to the dreaming and scheming of other men. That irritated her.

Bouncing along in the wagon, Elisabeth's impatience with James caused her to grumble a bit to herself and reflect how desperately she wanted to talk to him privately; to share all the triumphs and troubles she'd gone through, the loneliness and fear, to tell him how she had survived and provided for their baby through the many long months. Over their first supper, the Elliotts and Briggs had started relaying to James some of the deprivation and difficulties Elisabeth and her "lost wagon train" had endured. Yet, after that brief bit of sharing, Elisabeth still had so much more left to tell James. Her many strong but private feelings were just starting to bubble up inside her. Her unexpressed feelings about the hardships of traveling out west as an inexperienced mother, all alone with her in-laws and a toddler. Surprisingly, she now realized that, apparently, she'd kept much buried deep inside her, and she greatly yearned for a chance to share it all with him. But when would she get her chance?

Another truth also gnawed at her. Except for the proceeds she received from selling their Missouri farm, they were still without any financial means. James had gone off in search of his gold and wealth, talking about the nice house he would have built with a new stove, by the time she got out there. In reality, he had spent it all on his long round trip back to the East looking for her. Now, he didn't even have a horse to his name! Thank heavens, she'd saved around $15.00 from the farm sale. That would help. It was hard to admit, but she resented that her dreamer of a husband was still without any money. The past two years of their stressful and painful separation had not helped them financially. Their only hope was the larger amount of farmland they soon would eventually own. Yes, they were finally all together again, but homeless and poor! How long would it take to put their lives back together?

She was startled by a loud snore from little Charles who was cuddled against her chest. Awakened from her thoughts now in the silence that had overtaken both adults, she stared at her husband.

Sensing her eyes on him, James turned his tanned face towards her and grinned. "We're doing it, Lizzie! Soon we're going to be visiting the other Bushnells on their own homesteads—Jason's, Helen's, Cory's, and Ma's. And then, it'll be our turn to claim our very own land." He took a big breath. "God has definitely protected and guided us, especially while we were apart. Though, I was just thinking how much effort it's taken for each of us to make it out here safely."

He seemed to be in a reflective mood. She instantly sensed this was her chance to talk seriously with him and she seized it. "It sure has! If you can sit still long enough, I'd like you to listen to me about all that," she replied. The sharp tone in these words stunned even her.

His grin was instantly gone. After a quiet pause, he asked "Well then, what is it you want to tell me? We've still got miles to go before getting to Grand Prairie, so I can sit still."

Given such a perfect opportunity, she was strangely hesitant. She took a deep breath and then once she got started, the words poured out. "Well, running the farm and trying to produce any decent crops back home was either much harder than you'd imagined, or you didn't want to tell me it would be so hard. You promised me that Jason and Cory would come help, and they did come regularly, but most of the burden fell on me. You know, they had their own farm and stock to take care of and their own family responsibilities."

"And then we had such a terribly wet spring, and the rain went on for months and months after you left us. That made the summer extremely short, and all crops were poor. Then, our next winter was even worse. I was so lonely and the weather so dreary, I must confess that I cried a lot. About then, Jason and Mother started talking about us all just quitting our farms and coming out here to look for you. Everyone was concerned. We hadn't heard anything from you."

She choked up on those last words and she had to pause to get her voice settled down.

However, without much control, she blurted, "You left me alone! You left me with our infant son and the whole farm to run. You left us and we never heard from you again. Just like that you were gone, and I had no idea when I'd ever see you again. Or, if I would ever see you again! I'm so angry at you, James. It was so hard while you were gone. Then on our way out here, we ran into so many dangers amongst our struggling wagon train. I wasn't even sure any of us were going to survive wandering around lost in the desert. Especially my baby! How could you do that to me?" she ended with a sob.

Elisabeth's anguished words were startling. It was obvious now that she'd kept her dark fears shoved down inside. She had bottled up so much, that now it all was just starting to spew out. Yes, she and little Charles had survived, but it had worn hard on her.

There was an awkward silence between them, now that she was done.

When James replied, it wasn't with words. They both watched the nearby hawk swoop down into the grass and fly back up again with a mouse or something small in its claws. Then, James reached over and covered her hand with his own. He let her continue to cry. Charles woke up during his mother's crying and started whimpering, too. Finally, James broke into all their tearful sounds with, "I wondered about all that many a time myself. While I was out here trying to be a miner, I wondered what you were feeling and how were you going to manage alone?" He paused. "I don't know what to say. I felt so stuck and hopeless farming back there in Kirksville. And then I got out here without you and our son, and many times I felt stuck and hopeless out here, too. I wasn't much of a gold miner, I learned that for sure."

He solemnly turned to face her. She kept her eyes downcast. "Elisabeth, look at me, please," he pleaded.

He waited until she turned her face back to him and could look him in the eye. Then slowly and deliberately he said, "I will never purposely leave you and our children again. I promise that, with God's help, I will stay beside you through the rest of our lives."

"Do you really mean that?" she softly questioned him. Her expression was doubtful, yet her voice sounded hopeful at the same time.

"I really do mean it."

# CHAPTER THREE

*Cory (John Corydon) Bushnell,*
*youngest brother of James*

## OCTOBER 1853

JASON AND MARTHA'S BABY girl was born the day after the Bushnells arrived in Springfield. The new "Uncle Cory" exclaimed "what timing that little one has!" She'd waited through the rough and terrible times of their near starvation and many struggles on the lost wagon train. It seemed this baby girl had just waited patiently until she could enter life in the comforts of the Briggs' home in Springfield. The grateful new parents named her Helen, after their older sister. Cory mused that was probably because Helen had been so helpful to tired, pregnant Martha on their long, arduous journey out west.

Understandably, the new mother and the grandmother were exhausted. The trip had taken so much longer than expected and had ended with the traumatic few weeks of being lost and hungry. Then, immediately after being rescued, came this exciting but tiring new little one's birth. However, even with just two days' rest after arriving, Jason, Helen, Edward, and Cory were too eager to sit around any longer. They needed to see what kind of claims could be found in this beautiful new land. All around them the autumn landscape displayed low hills covered by ash, alder, and some cedar trees, with scatterings of brilliant gold and orange maple trees clustered there and about. They were on the threshold of their year-long dream, and now some of this lush-looking land was about to become theirs! The two women completely surprised them, though. Apparently, they were just as eager to finally get settled in one place, because by the time the men were ready to go, Martha and Mother Bushnell were ready to come along, too—new baby and all! They understood just how anxious the men were to start looking for claims.

So, after laying over just two days in Springfield, all seven Bushnells took off again. The group left Elisabeth and little Charles Alvah with the Briggs family in hopes that James could find them more easily there. The others headed towards the open fields and plains to the west in search of open land claims. Having recently come through the coarse, dry, rocky desert of central Oregon, they eagerly scanned the flat, fertile valley ahead.

Cory marveled to Jason, "Who knew we'd be able to see for miles in this open country? This vast prairie is unlike any I've ever seen in my 20 years. And see the land isn't covered by the usual thick, tough turf either. Instead, it looks like it's ready and waiting to be cultivated with little effort."

Jason replied, "Yep. They weren't wrong telling us the soil was rich and dark. Even this late in autumn, there's still plenty of green to be seen. And those colored fall leaves are spectacular to behold! It is nice that so many trees still have their leaves."

Driving their covered wagon farther along, they were surprised that so many families already camped out on plots. Whenever they stopped to ask about any of the land surrounding those camps, they always heard "already taken." And many claims were being saved for extended family members who were expected to arrive anytime. The Bushnells' hopes started faltering as they passed through miles and miles of these "already claimed" fields.

It finally occurred to Cory how many other wagon trains had come before them and now here those folks were getting the best land ahead of him! That discouraged him and he spoke out. "I'm afraid we're only going to get a Hobson's choice (or the only choice left) for the three claims we need."

Nobody argued with him, but instead quietly nodded their heads. They camped for the night along the beach of what they heard was called Clear Lake. Getting up to frost on the ground, they shook off the cold and quickly agreed to eat a cold breakfast of biscuits and boiled eggs and get on their ride again soon. Heading mostly eastwards now and somewhat to the north, they learned they were in what's was named Grand Prairie by some others.

By this time, they had all learned to spot likable land, but without getting their hopes up. At least, Cory did. That morning they found some flat, browning grassland that was available! However, it wasn't very appealing to him, even though these two unclaimed plots were the sizes they needed.

He voiced his complaint, "This area isn't as scenic as I've been dreaming about. Where are the rolling green meadows with creeks running through them?" Again, no one answered him.

Nonetheless, there was a dribble of a creek and a few mud puddles discovered by Jason on one piece which meant a spring might possibly be lying nearby. Their mother was always the most practical of the bunch. She firmly declared to all, "Water will come with the rains— and hard work will make the soil productive."

With that said, Jason, Martha and Mother agreed to mark these two plots but to also keep on looking. Cory had some say in this, but as he was underaged, his land claim could only be in Mother's name.

Sister Helen and her husband Edward weren't so sure and decided they were going to keep heading farther to the southwest. So, all of them agreed to go on searching together still. After marking these two plots with string on four approximate spots that they hoped were corners, they continued across the Grand Prairie. When they stopped to check on other pieces of land, they always got the same answer as the day before— "already taken."

Another night of camping found the Bushnell clan in the Fern Ridge area, still looking for their elusive perfect pieces of vacant land. Helen and Edward considered one unclaimed piece of land and the others watched as they looked it over. It wasn't bad, and they only needed one piece, so it made sense that they might want it. But it meant living quite a bit away from the rest of their family. Nobody brought that up, though, as they watched the Adkins do their considering.

"We would only be a few hours away by wagon," Helen said wistfully. And with that, they decided to take it. The others helped them unpack their belongings and set up the tent they'd been lugging along. Then they all celebrated by spending the night with them and excitedly imagining aloud how this place would become Helen and Edward's new home.

It was on the third day, or the next day, that the rest of the Bushnells stopped heading west and started angling back towards the Grand Prairie area. This time when they arrived back at the plots they'd marked two days earlier, the three others listened to Mother's opinion. They all watched her carefully use some charcoal to print "Bushnell" on a piece of dishrag she had torn into wide strips. This time they more clearly marked the two claims, by tying these rags onto young trees and shrubs throughout the property. . . Jason and Martha claimed their 640 acres and Mother claimed her 320 acres as a single person. Since Cory was too young to make a claim, they marked the remaining 320 acres for James and Elisabeth, just in case James couldn't find anything larger or better.

They camped again for the third night with Mother, Martha, and in-fant Helen in the wagon and Jason and Cory on the ground nearby. Cory said "Good night, all. For the first time, we're actually bedding down on our new land! What a great feeling and I don't even mind the bumpy ground." He heard happy, contented murmurs in response.

In the morning, the first thing they did was begin piecing together a shanty on Mother's claim. The two sons dragged small fallen branches and rotting wood over to make a wind break with three corners. Then they cut boughs with leaves still attached from a nearby ash tree to put up and over the canvas the women had taken off their wagon. Mother had put it up as a cover and it became the roof. It was her idea that putting the ash boughs over the canvas would protect the shelter some from the coming rains. She'd scraped a fire pit near the edges of this lean-to, while the others constructed some rough outlines for walls from larger branches found in clumps of nearby foliage. Then, after she piled up smaller pieces of wood, Mother got out their precious tinderbox. It had traveled with her from New York to Missouri and then the whole Oregon Trail. All the others watched her striking as she said she was "going to get the home fire burning." Cory and the others heartedly cheered when that fire caught on!

# CHAPTER FOUR

## *James and Elisabeth*

JAMES AND ELISABETH LEFT the Briggs' place in Springfield knowing only that their family hoped to claim two or three plots in the Grand Prairie area. And that they were hoping to be near the McClure family, her dear wagon train friends.

The little family of three had already bumped along about fifteen miles northwest of Springfield, and they kept praying they were getting close. They beseeched God to help them finish their journey well—and soon! They encountered quite a few wagons, shanties, or lean-tos with new settlers occupying most of the land already. The sun was high on the second day when they found a fresh horse-and-wagon trail wandering across an open grassy field. But there were no tents, lean-tos, or fence posts in sight. James took that rough trail on a whim, and soon Elisabeth spied some rags fluttering in the breeze, tied to a few elderberry bushes. James drove up as close as he could get their wagon. Elizabeth made sure their little boy was still sleeping and jumped out to check what the tags read. When Elizabeth first made out the word "Bushnell," she started to shout, "We're here! We've found them!" — and climbed back up in the wagon.

Immediately, James began joyfully hollering out, "Hey, Bushnells!" repeatedly and loudly. Then James urged the startled and confused little Charles to help with their shouting, too. Both parents laughed at their little one's "Hey, Bushels! Hey, Bushels!"

Driving carefully along the rough trail, they continued shouting and finally heard some responding "Heys" coming back at them. Soon, they could see family members waving enthusiastically at them across the field of tall grasses. It quickly became obvious that the other Bushnells recognized James riding beside Elisabeth, as they started yelling his name and running toward the wagon! James recklessly urged the team to go faster, causing Elisabeth to tighten her hold both on Charles and the wagon seat.

Stopping the wagon amongst the waving and cheering greeters, James quickly jumped down, taking Charles from Elisabeth's arms, and setting his son down gently. Once the toddler was on his own two little feet, Mother Bushnell grabbed James and hugged him tightly for a long, long time. Then his brothers, Jason, and Corydon, each had a turn. Jason proudly introduced his brand-new daughter, asleep in Martha's arms despite the ruckus. Only Helen and Edward were missing from this happy reunion. James soon learned that they had settled on a claim a bit farther to the west. Elisabeth found herself weeping a bit at the happy family reunion scene unfolding before her. During all this excitement, and commotion, young Charles stared from the sidelines. Then, probably from his perceived lack of attention, he started crying louder and louder: "Mama! Mama!" Elisabeth quickly alighted from her seat, swept him up in her arms and began consoling him.

As he slowly walked the horses and wagon back towards the Bushnells' camp, James was bombarded with questions. He shook his head more than once, "I still can't believe you didn't get my journal or any of the letters I sent back to Missouri! I sure hope they're not lost forever."

His mother quickly made sure that James and Elisabeth knew there was an adjoining half-claim already staked out for their family.

"Now, that's a great relief, just in case everything else nearby is taken," James said enthusiastically, and clapped the back of his nearest brother.

Then he went back to answering all their many questions. In a bit, he abruptly declared, "Hey! I found William in the gold hills outside of Shasta City, California. Buddy Tim and I accidentally ran into William and some of his mining pals on the very same trail. It was a remarkable reunion that only God could have managed. So, Tim and I mined with William all that winter." He directed all this news to his mother because William had left home a year before James, and no one else in the family had heard a word from this oldest son in the past two years. James knew that had been especially hard on his mother.

That good news caused everyone to suddenly stop talking and they simply stood amazed upon hearing of James' chance encounter with William. It was Mother who first broke the silence. "Oh, dear God, thank you for watching over my two lost boys all this time! Father, you are so good to us." Several voices echoed "Amen" after her grateful words. She gripped James again and melted into his arms. He held her tightly as he wasn't sure she was able to stand on her own at that moment. When she finally pulled away, James had to wipe his own tears away on his jacket sleeve. Then he offered the same sleeve to his mother, too. This made Mother chuckle and the whole family began to laugh along.

After they all found a log, a barrel, or the wagon tongue to sit on, James began to describe the harsh winter he, his good friend and mining partner Tim, and William spent together at William's camp. "We were all mining Williams claim. Or rather, trying to gold mine!" James added ruefully. He went on to describe Tim's eventual impatience and deep discouragement that finally caused him to leave the two Bushnell brothers, totally give up on mining, and head on towards San Francisco.

Then, slowly, and with a few furtive glances at Elisabeth, James began to reveal his own months of loneliness and depression, which led him to eventually give up mining with William, also. As soon as the spring weather permitted, William took off for the Sacramento River area and James took off in the opposite direction, determined to collect his gold from the Shasta City Bank and immediately head back to Kirksville and his family. Thus began a dangerous and terrible time for him

That was seven long months ago now.

# CHAPTER FIVE

## *James and Elisabeth settle their own claim*

AWARE THAT WINTER WAS rapidly approaching, James and Elisabeth needed to quickly decide about the half plot near his mother and Cory. They decided to ride over to the neighboring claims and see if they could find any other half or whole plots adjoining the Bushnells. To their amazement there was a single man from Elisabeth's wagon train on a whole 360-acre plot just to the north. With a conversation that started friendly, Elisabeth listened to James' voice grow firmer and firmer as he reminded this neighbor he could get government men to come impose the official claiming rights, if needed. The younger man conceded half of his claim easily after that. The two men shook hands and then discussed where to draw the property line.

While the men rode off on horses to decide, Elisabeth walked with little Charles around in the area. She watched her little boy pick up rocks and sticks and delight in the bugs he found. When she looked up and stood to admire the sun descending near the western hills, Charles got farther away from her. When she stopped her daydreaming and turned, he was running quickly away. She called "Charles Alva, come back over here." He stopped and grinned at her as if to say, "Mama, you need to chase me!" and turned and started trotting away again. She sighed and called again, "Charlie, come to Mama and see this bug I found," while walking quickly towards him. He didn't even acknowledge her and kept on going on his short little legs. And, just as she feared, down he crashed into the brush and dirt! He wasn't laughing anymore, now, but hollering and crying instead. Briskly walking over to him, she picked him up and gently brushed off his hands and knees. In a soothing voice she said, "There. There. I wish you'd stay close to Mama and not run so fast." Knowing she was probably wasting her breath, she carried him back to the wagon and planned to put him inside. However, Charles protested by kicking and yelling, "No more wagon! I want down!" So, she sat him down close to her, reached into the wagon seat and got out some bread and water.

"Here, Charles. Let's have a little picnic. You can choose where we will sit?" He nodded to her, and she followed as he led them to a smooth, grassy spot the horses had trodden down.

He turned and looked up at his mother, asking "Do you like this ground, Mama?" She smiled at his sudden cooperativeness and said, "I like it very much."

They ate, and he kept on his search for bugs all around their spot. Soon, he laid his head in his mother's lap and she stroked his light brown hair. This was the peaceful scene that James and neighbor Brown found upon riding back.

The men had worked out an agreement on the boundary, so next, James wanted to drive Elisabeth around and see if they could quickly decide where to put up their cabin. He hoped to have made the choice before sundown, if possible. Together they drove the wagon once around their property and then walked part of it. James had to carry his sleepy son. After surveying parts of their new and unknown land on foot, they agreed on a flat spot that was already partially cleared out and not too far from Mother Bushnell's trickle of mud and water. "It's probably just a seasonal creek," James reckoned. With this, their decision was made easily enough.

It was already getting quite chilly out in the prairie wind. Around the cheery campfire eating a cold meal on their own land, Elisabeth said she understood their home would have to be small and rough, given the urgency. He was glad she agreed. In a few minutes, James suggested, "Why don't you and Charles spend a few more weeks at the Briggs' while I help Cory and Jason get their cabins framed with the walls and roof up. Then when their cabins are good enough, I'm sure they'll help me get ours ready—to stand against the rain and wind, at least."

Elisabeth didn't respond to his idea right away. He watched her solemnly as she weighed the idea in her mind. He imagined she was thinking that the Briggs had a nice, warm home and the extra room for her and the lad.

Elisabeth finally spoke. "What if Charles and I stayed there one more week while you help the rest of the family finish building? Along the way, perhaps you men can find and cut the trees we need for our cabin, too. After that week, I'll come back out here and help with some of the hauling. I can at least help shave off tree bark. Charles can play nearby and then nap while I work on cleaning the logs. I'd like to help build our home, too. Also, James, I think we've already been apart much too long." She said that quite definitely.

"You're right there," he replied, smiling at her. "I think that's a good idea and it may not even take me a whole week to do what I need. Maybe I can come get you sooner."

She smiled in response and reached for his hand. "Sooner would be nice."

The next day James returned his little family to the Briggs' house along with the wagon he'd borrowed. Then in return, he borrowed two work horses and the necessary rigging to haul logs. Although he also needed another riding horse, he was reluctant to ask, since he felt already deeply in debt to the generous Briggs family. When he finally made himself ask for the extra horse, Elias Briggs simply said, "That's what this homesteading is all about." Back home James knew this kind of generosity was called "community" and it seemed to be working out here, too. People were helping others get settled in any way they could.

# CHAPTER SIX

## *Homesteading*

"UGH! FRESHLY CUT WOOD weighs more than I remember. It's so wet and heavy," James complained as he and Jason started moving the first logs they'd cut. The Bushnell brothers were not big men, but they were strong. With all three brothers working on the first two cabins, the walls and door frames went up fairly well. The cabins were barely more than closed-in shanties, but they were a good start.

On the sixth day, it was their turn to help James cut the oak trees he'd selected from the nearest woods. He'd chosen logs as straight as possible to make snug fitting walls. He'd also measured the best trees to make logs about 15 feet long. Then, he'd found some others that were closer to 20 feet long. He and Jason got started cutting those down while Cory rigged up the horses in preparation for pulling the logs over to James' site. After bringing the horses up close, Cory helped strip off branches from the freshly hewn trees.

James also found some smaller trees perfect for the rafters. They'd make poles measuring about 20 feet long. It took two days to cut these logs of varying sizes and widths. Most of his logs were at the cabin site, but some were still lying exactly where they fell. James knew this was when Elisabeth would like to help, so he separated himself from his brothers and took one horse back to the Briggs'. It was time to collect Elisabeth and little Charles.

Back at the Briggs' he was greeted warmly and with much interest. Everyone wanted to know how the camping and cabin building was going. Mrs. Briggs and the other women put together a special dinner, a farewell of sorts, although they knew they would always be neighbors. And that was a comfort and a blessing— especially to Elisabeth. The next morning after the Bushnells slept their last night in the Briggs' comfortable and lovely home, they loaded all they could pack onto the borrowed wagon and the little family of three rode together to their new home on Grand Prairie. The sun was out and about mid-high when they arrived. Elisabeth set Charles down to play in the outline of logs that made their foundation and then she walked around the outline. James said, "I am making it 20 by 15. Not very big, but we can get it done quickly and easily add on or enlarge it later."

"Oh, don't worry, James, I wasn't going to complain. I'm very happy to see this good start." Then Elisabeth set some of their loose cookware inside the log framework, to keep Charles busy for a bit.

Now, she felt ready to help start shaving bark off the limbs. Together they surveyed the logs already atop the sawhorse that James and his brothers had put together. James used the ax, and she used the hatchet. Once Elisabeth was well underway and Charles was busy trying to catch worms and bugs off the stacked logs, James left her to work alone. He took one horse and rode off to let his other family know they were back now. Then, he took off alone to finish cleaning off and dragging their roof poles. A 20-foot log was definitely more weight than he could drag alone, but with the horse, he could manage one pole at a time.

When he was done piling up his 20-foot rafters along one side of the cabin, he joined Elisabeth again in peeling off bark. She smiled in gratitude. She paused and stretched. "Obviously, I need to fix some food for our fussy little boy. I'd love it if I could get him to nap here, but that may be a lost cause. I can't figure out any way to corral him enough that gets him settled down. He's eager to explore everything new and I suppose that's natural," she sighed. "Hopefully, he'll give-in to sleep soon enough."

She brought out some of the ham sandwiches she'd packed up back at the Briggs' and they stopped to eat among the pungent bark shavings and rough logs. Charles mostly tore up his bread but was content. Elisabeth handed a water cup to the little boy, and he held it with his two dimpled little hands and gulped a few times. James took the water cup from him and finished it off.

Standing, James offered Elisabeth his hand and pulled her up from the low log. They both knew they had to keep working until sundown or until Charles complained too much. Between the two of them, they finished shaving off two of the long logs and four of the shorter ones that day. James notched each log as well as he could to make corners that fit together. Then, he and Elisabeth together managed to carry each heavy, wet log from the see saws and lay them end-to-end in their rectangular plot, starting the frame of their new cabin. They worked until dusk and ate more of the ham sandwiches.

Without a door cut out yet, they each had to step or crawl over the logs to lay out their bedding inside on the wild grass. In one corner, Elisabeth made a small enclosure for Charles to bed in, using their travel bags and a couple of barrels. She held him and sang to him enough, so the little one's eyes got sleepy. When she thought it was time, she sat him down inside his little pen. She and James held their breath, but Charles just settled down with a deep sigh.

Then she snuggled down next to James' warm prone body and they each sighed again, this time contentedly. "We're finally alone. Just our family," she murmured.

"Exactly what I was thinking," James replied. "And look at that full moon peeking through the clouds at us. It's the same moon whether we're in Missouri or Oregon. It's the same God looking over us, too. That's my comfort, Lizzie, as we start out with so much work to get done ahead of us. God is still the same God. His love and wisdom are ours everyday wherever we go."

She fell asleep admiring the moon and enjoying the wind brushing through the tall grasses around her.

Elisabeth's next day started with the happy sound of chirping birds and then the "Mama! Mama!" of an unhappy little Charles. James stirred and stretched beside her as she sat up and crawled over to the toddler's enclosure. The lad wanted out! She could see that his bedding was wet, and he'd soaked through his rags, too. "It's okay, Charlie boy. You can get out and I'll make you dry and happy soon. Just stand still another minute," she encouraged him as she removed his wet clothes in the chilly morning air. The two-and-a-half-year-old wiggled, squirmed, and protested all the while.

James chuckled, "You might as well let him air dry out here. No one's going to see or mind. I'll get the fire going and find that coffee you packed yesterday. I've gained a few cooking skills since I've been on my own for so long," he joked.

After their breakfast of cold hardboiled eggs, bread, and coffee, it was time to get back to work. James started shaving another one of the long logs and when Elisabeth was able to join him, he asked her to work on the other end. He cut out the notches on both ends and they both finished the debarking in the middle. Then they hoisted their finished log and set it on the awaiting shorter log. One by one, in this manner, their walls went up. When all four walls were up to waist height, James decided it was time to cut out the door opening. Swinging his ax, he made cuts about two and a half feet apart and as evenly as possible. Elisabeth helped him remove the chunks of wood that were left lying about. She coaxed Charles into helping her pick up the small bits and pieces around, too. That kept the toddler busy for a few minutes, at least. The rest of the morning was spent shaving, notching, and stacking two more logs. Stooping through the half door to get out, James declared their noon break. Elisabeth had already taken a few breaks due to tending Charles as he played or fell, cried, or got hungry. They all took their apples and bread away from the cabin and sat on a nice patch of green grass.

It was a cloudy day, but not cold. Once done eating, James carried Charles on his shoulders, and they all walked through the grassy field. They stopped by some of the stumps in the tree line, which were still too pitchy to sit on, but provided some good back rests with a pleasant view ahead. Husband and wife sat and watched their busy little boy follow bugs and butterflies in the grass. Charles chortled and delighted himself with these discoveries and his delight made his parents laugh, too. Too soon, James declared "Back to work!" And he and Elisabeth got up and stretched. They walked back to their half-finished cabin. James started notching the next log. Elisabeth put a quilt down on a smooth spot near them and set Charles down to rest. He had some rocks they'd found and his baby doll to play with. He was thoroughly enjoying banging the rocks together to make noises, stacking them, and knocking them down.

As the walls went up higher and higher, Elisabeth was soon at a disadvantage. Neither she nor James were tall, but she couldn't reach like he could and get the logs up over her shoulders. James took the horse and rode off to get Jason and Cory's help. After the men arrived and they got three more high rounds done, they decided the cabin was tall enough for this winter. They could always go higher when the spring came if they wanted.

Elisabeth had fixed a campfire and warmed the remaining ham from Mary Briggs for the two brothers to share with them. The men exclaimed it tasted delicious, but Charles fussed at it. He got another egg for dinner. After the meal, Jason and Cory returned to their family and James finished chopping out the rest of the door. He worked until he had a nice, even-sided, fairly smooth opening on both sides and across the top. Then, Elisabeth helped James choose the best poles from his pile for their rafters. Lifting these smaller poles together was easier for Elisabeth, especially as her arms had rested a bit. They got the ten poles laid up on the old canvas they'd stretched across the top logs. On the canvas, they just rolled them into place. After the last pole was up, they both stepped back to look and then grinned at each other. They had a cabin with a roof! And it wasn't even quite dark yet.

Elisabeth hung a blanket for their door. "Now, I feel as secure as a bug-in-a-rug." They slept under a roof that night and dreamed of being off the ground soon.

# CHAPTER SEVEN

THE NEXT DAY THEY rode the horses to the nearly dry creek in search for small muddy stones and water, and hopefully wood for puncheons. The water would be used to make mud. Then, the mud and rocks would make insulation between the cabin's logs. When they got close to the tiny creek, James was excited to see that someone had already cut some wider trees and left a few of them. He found one he could use to make the puncheons for their floor. Loading up the gravel and stones in a canvas bag, James slung the bag over one saddle horn. He set Elisabeth on that horse with the two large pans of water in her lap. They joked about how wet she was going to be!

"I sure hope there will be some water left by the time we get to the cabin," she laughed.

James grabbed Charles and set him on the other saddle up near the horn and sternly told him to hold onto it and sit still. Then, James grabbed the bucket full of water and swung himself astride the horse trying to keep the bucket balanced. Of course, some sloshed out, but they started back to the cabin as best they could. For awhile, Charles whined over leaving his new muddy playground behind. James soon distracted him with a silly song about a bucket full of water.

Elisabeth's upper skirt was soaked before they made it back, but they had much of the water still. After careful unloading, they looked over their cabin. They decided that while James went back with a horse and harness to get the log, Elisabeth would begin working on the ground inside the cabin.

Soon after James left, Elisabeth began scraping up the grass and weeds inside with a small branch. She scratched away until she could pull up the loose grass and toss it out the door. Charles laughed whenever she threw out a pile and he pulled the long wild grass around like a toy. Eventually

Elisabeth cleared the grass down to the dirt. She invited Charles inside and showed him how to loosen the dirt with a stick and help her make a dirty floor. Cheerfully they worked alongside each other. However, it wasn't long before the little boy tired of the game and began to cry for them "to stop working."

Giving up, Elisabeth fixed them a quick lunch and they rested for a bit. Charles was reluctant to sit down, but she picked him up and insisted he come sit beside her and eat, too. While eating his bread, he soon leaned against her and hadn't finished even half before he was asleep. She was able to gently lay him down in the grass and get back to her work.

With a tin bowl, she began scraping up their loosened dirt and pounding out the clumps. James had been gone a good hour or more but returned triumphant. With the log now lying near the cabin, he began splitting it lengthwise using the flat rock he'd found as a wedge and split some rough, thick boards.

That woke Charles up and the little one cried and wailed. Soon, though, he was caught up in the mud making activity of his mother's. He wasn't about to be left out of that fun and clamored to "help her make mud." Obliging, she got down the smaller pan and using a tin cup she added some of their dirt and showed him how to stir with his own stick. James grinned at his little family making mud together.

When the mother and child got the dirt floor all muddy at least two inches down, the split logs were laid in place one at a time onto their new mud. Once three planks were heaved and shoved down onto moistened dirt, Elisabeth and James carefully worked with the planks settling them into place. Then James encouraged little Charles to run all over them, to help pack them down. Surprised, the lad walked gingerly on a plank and soon started laughing at his parents' silly antics. Understanding they actually wanted him to walk or run all over the wood with them, he was happy to oblige!

James thought the floor was securely done not long after that. However, Elisabeth said with a smile to her husband, "I will be the one sweeping it," and she reached for the hatchet and started smoothing out the boards some more. By midday, apparently satisfied with her floor, she murmured "That's better now."

James held Charles as he smiled and said, "All that is left now is the door, and then I'll feel as snug as a bug-in-a-rug, too." Setting the boy down, he picked up two shorter planks left over from the floor and cut them to fit the door. He roped them together in two spots as tightly as possible. "When we get some leather, you know I'll redo this door for you, right?" he said to Elizabeth who just nodded her assent. She was resting and watching him work.

Next, he pushed the two poles chosen for door framing into each side of his door opening, settling them into the dips he'd dug on each side. With Elisabeth helping, they heaved the door into place and roped it. As she helped hold it in place, James tied the rope ends onto the right-side pole. It was demanding work and they needed to adjust the rope more than once, but finally it was just high enough to swing over the front clearing. They both cheered at this successful final step and then sank down to sit on their floor, backs against the wall. James coaxed little Charles to clap his hands and the child enthusiastically did it.

"In this apology for a house, we'll spend our first winter in Oregon," declared James.

# CHAPTER EIGHT

DURING THEIR FIRST LONG and dreary winter in Oregon, Elisabeth grew discouraged with the constant gray: gray sky, gray landscape, gray clouds. The dull winter seemed like an endless parade of cloudy days —whether it rained or not. And it usually rained!

As spring started to arrive, she noticed and welcomed each bit of color. During breaks between the spring rains, she urged the little family to take some day trips in the Bushnell family wagon. She declared these outings as "looking for Spring trips." They got excited when they spotted buds on trees blooming and found budding daffodils!

It was their first spring when James found a piece of land he liked better. It had a few nice shade trees, less dense grass to plow up, more green meadows and not far from a decent creek. Right after discovering that this land was available, he happily returned home. Finding Elisabeth at the cook stove, he began describing it enthusiastically.

Elisabeth turned and wiped her hands on her apron. He was shocked when, instead of being excited, she began to complain. "James, you are such a dreamer. You should have warned me that you're never satisfied to stay long in one place."

Caught off guard, he stammered, "I thought you'd be happy to get into a better place."

"I've learned to adjust in each place we've lived and make the most of it." She swept her arms around and stated, "This cabin isn't so bad. I dread the work of building another one. I have no energy or enthusiasm to do it again. I would much rather settle down and stay put for a while."

The dreamer didn't give up his plan, though. It wasn't long before James convinced her to go see this new plot of land. Next, he convinced her they could just move their cabin, instead of starting construction all over again, by putting some runners under their house and letting the horses pull it to the new land. And that's just what they did!

So, on a cool, but dry Saturday in March, James invited Cory, Jason, and Elias Briggs to their mostly empty cabin. The men walked around studying the cabin walls. Then, Jason and Cory helped Elisabeth remove the last and heaviest furniture from the inside. That was the rough bedframe and handmade table. She and James had already packed a barrel full of dishes, pots, and all their clothing. A bucket was filled with little Charles' clothes and a few toys. All the other miscellaneous household items were in some baskets. The wagon already held their farming tools and the three chairs James had made. Elisabeth had tied up the bedding and her few towels into a big bundle that Cory tossed into the wagon for her.

James and Elias left to look for some good poles to use for the lifting and hauling of the cabin. Finding and cutting three ash poles about 22 feet long, they hauled them back to the cabin. While James and Jason took to smoothing off the few knots on each pole and stripping the bark, the others enjoyed some hot coffee and warm biscuits Elisabeth provided. Once the poles had been smoothed and they were all refreshed, they were ready to go. Elisabeth and Charles stood off to the side watching the process unfold. It took three men to lift one cabin corner off the ground. Then as quickly as he could, Cory slid the first long, narrow pole under that hefted corner as far as possible. Setting their raised log corner gently down on the pole, the three men slowly stood, stretched their backs, and moved over to the opposite end. Here it was more challenging. Once they heaved this corner up, Cory had to scoot underneath as far as he could to reach that same pole and pull it to the far corner. This took more time with the three huffing and puffing as they kept the corner raised and safely away from smashing Cory underneath it. Once that corner of the cabin was above the pole, they slowly and cautiously lowered that corner. Everyone held their breath as they set this whole cabin side on the single pole, hoping the pole stayed in place and didn't break. Relieved to see it held both corners without cracking, all the lifters cheered! They stretched their back muscles again and paced around in small circles.

It was Jason who first noticed a group of three horseback riders approaching. More neighbors were coming to help. The Briggs had spread the word! Not only did the newly arrived men offer their help, but they also informed Elisabeth that the women were preparing a picnic over at the new place. The spread of food should be waiting for them by the time they arrived with their traveling cabin.

Now they had four strong men to lift the third corner. Once those men lifted the house at the corner, two others guided the second pole as far as they could underneath the raised structure. Isaac Briggs, the oldest of the men, became the supervisor and shouted out directions to them. Task accomplished. After resting a bit, they tackled the fourth and final corner. They all shouted loudly with relief and pride as the last corner balanced nicely and the whole cabin was sitting on the two bottom rails. The clamor startled young Charles. The little boy's alarmed cries quickly stopped, however, when he saw how happy the grownups were.

Cory and James were nominated to slide the third pole between the existing two already holding up the cabin, while the others began the work of fashioning two slabs of wood for crosspieces to secure the ends of the three poles. It didn't take James and Cory long to shove their central runner into place and it was ready to be secured to the crosspieces. James had invested in some nails from the blacksmith which he and Jason used to secure the three runners to the crosspieces both in front and back of the cabin. Cheers went up again when that was finished! Their house was now on skids and ready for the move! But first, more of Elisabeth's biscuits and coffee. . . .

Elisabeth and James packed the Bushnell family's wagon with their final belongings. When the wagon was ready to move out, with Elisabeth and little Charles as passengers, Cory climbed up on the bench. James had put him in charge of driving the two horses and wagon. To move the empty house, James had borrowed a team of two oxen. He now hitched them to the front crosspiece.

Heading out on what they hoped was the smoothest route, they all started east to the Bushnell's new land claim. Their friends and neighbors all rode slowly on ahead, looking for potential problems and shouting directions back to James, who was cautiously driving the team pulling the cabin. They were all trying to avoid as many of the obvious obstacles as possible. Jason rode his horse behind the cabin watching for trouble from back there. In this mostly unsettled, untilled land, plenty of brush, small trees and undergrowth couldn't be avoided. It was rough going. Mr. Briggs and Jason coaxed and prodded the team over some of the unavoidable troublesome spots, many times guiding the lead horse and ox by their bits while walking alongside them. Dragging the cabin over the bumpy ground left deep, muddy ruts as they scraped along.

The moving process was slow, but at least the weather held fair and dry. All the movers exhaled a big mutual sigh of relief when they actually arrived at the new plot with the cabin still intact. Before they stopped to be greeted by the friendly group waiting for them, Elisabeth assertively directed the men as to where the cabin should sit and where to face its only door. She definitely preferred her door facing west to catch the afternoon sun. She'd already discovered the joy of pausing to watch the many beautiful sunsets in this lovely, flat land rimmed with low western mountains. Those coastal mountain ranges were breathtaking when silhouetted in the evening sunlight. Supervising from the ground, she got the men to set the cabin down properly in her chosen place and made sure it was firmly secure. Then she, too, could breathe a sigh of relief.

Several new neighbors and the Briggs women had spread out a supper for the Bushnells, the work crew, and their families to all enjoy. It became quite a party, with children laughing and chasing each other around in circles, women catching up with family and baby news, and men planning their spring crops. Elisabeth especially enjoyed the female companionship of Betsy and Mary Briggs. Even though she'd been living with her two sisters-in-law close by, she realized she still missed her other new friends.

# CHAPTER NINE

ALONE ONCE AGAIN, THE young couple dug out some of the grass in the nearest meadows surrounding the cabin site over the next few days. In these dark, moist plots, they planted oats and wheat, with seeds provided by Elias Briggs, who had also generously added a gift of two apple tree seedlings. Elisabeth let James know she wanted the trees to grow near the western side of the cabin so they would eventually provide some late afternoon shade.

By May they had a nice-sized garden planted, and their field crops were all in the ground. James spent that summer building fences around the fields to attempt to keep the deer out. They spent a pleasant summer watching their crops grow and pregnant Elisabeth's belly grow. Towards the end of that summer, they began to enjoy some of their own produce. But sadly, before they could get in most of their first harvest, the rains came. Heavy rain. The downpours kept coming for days that led into weeks. The rain destroyed much of their crops. Truly little could be saved. So now, just like that, their winter supplies looked bleak instead of encouraging. James declared that they were at God's mercy, and he trusted his loving God. This reassured Elisabeth.

A ray of light broke through their gloom when on Nov. 1, 1854, a baby girl was added to their family. Elisabeth and James named her Lucy Jennette. James had lost a sister named Jennette when he was seven years old and so he wanted their baby's name now to remember her. Three-year-old big brother Charles soon had them all calling the baby "Net." Elisabeth's labor and delivery had been long and the only woman who could get through to help, due to the rains and floods, was Betsy Briggs. She helped the little family with cooking, cleaning, and encouragement. She also taught James how to supplement Elisabeth's own meager milk supply with some goat's milk. After two days of this, the new baby stopped her crying and began to thrive. So, Elisabeth was able to relax, and soon her milk came in stronger. Betsy Briggs set off for home, reassuring them that she'd be happy to come back if she was needed.

The little Bushnell family settled into a somewhat smoother pace and could now delight more in this precious new baby. However, even all these joys were overshadowed by the grimness of the approaching winter and their meager supplies. Based on the harsh fall already upon them, the Bushnells and the other locals all feared a fiercely bitter winter was coming. It proved to be too much for Elisabeth to even think about, as she had two little ones to care for in their tiny cabin. James worried that she still looked weak and told her he couldn't imagine being cooped up with the little ones either. He'd have to give extra care for their animals too, if the weather predictions were correct. He did get Elisabeth to laugh once, when he said "I could survive in a tent cooking over a campfire for months in the gold fields without a care. Yet, the thought of being cooped up even just one month with two little ones as young as ours scares me to death!"

By the end of November, the family of four left their claim and headed back to the hills of Springfield. The continually generous Briggs family had offered them work and lodging through the winter. It was just the kind of help that James and Elisabeth needed for their family. James went to work in their sawmill and Elisabeth was hired to cook for the mill workers. James, who'd always been fascinated with the mechanics of the millrace, was eager to learn to work the sawmill and the grain mill. Elisabeth was happy to return to such a lovely, finished home and be with her friends again.

Sharing one small bedroom was only a minor inconvenience, especially after the cramped cabin they'd left behind. Elisabeth thoroughly enjoyed being back in Betsy Briggs' nice kitchen and being around her friends again. Graciously, all the Briggs took a three-year old and newborn baby in stride. The women kindly encouraged Elisabeth as she adjusted to caring for two little children. James' responsibilities at the mill were mostly relegated to daytime hours and that meant he could enjoy some family life, too. He hungrily admired the Briggs' three shelves of books and soon was encouraged to borrow them as often as he liked. Most every evening, once alone in their room, Elisabeth and he took turns reading to their little family. Then James continued reading to himself after the children were asleep. They also eagerly attended a weekly gathering of Christians on Sunday afternoons in the Briggs' home. Isaac and Elias Briggs were strong believers with a zeal for spreading God's word. James admired their spirituality and he watched how they lived every day. He was impressed with the loving kindness of the Briggs family and how they cared for any, and all, folks in need. He'd already noticed how all around them, most people were settling into a brand-new life with many needs, too.

In this cozy arrangement, the Bushnells spent six months at the Briggs home. When it came time to leave, they went home with two cows, quite a bit of lumber and a few tools they badly needed to fix up their little house.

Back on Grand Prairie, James got to work building their first barn. The Bushnell brothers, brother-in-law Edward and several neighbors came to help with their barn raising, and quickly up it went. That barn ended up being three times as big as their house and Elisabeth rarely let him forget it!

# CHAPTER TEN

It was now November of 1855. The harvest was set in, and the farmers could relax a bit. James was asked to meet with eight of the local men regarding planning a school for all their children. These men came calling one evening after supper. James welcomed his brother William first, who had moved his family up from California, then their good friend James McClure, from their wagon train, and six other friends. They crowded around the Bushnell table and after visiting over tea and cookies provided by Elisabeth, they got down to business. James McClure was first to speak and reviewed reasons why it seemed time to start the first school in that part of the county. Elisabeth had already told James that the women, back at their barn raising, had also discussed this. But James didn't have to be convinced by anyone, man or woman, as he was in total agreement in the need for a community school. Since he didn't need convincing, why were these men going on and on about it, he mused?

"Well, James, we'd like you to be the one to start up teaching the school," James McClure suddenly stated.

James was stunned. After a moment's pause, "I am flattered, but shocked," he responded. "I need some time to consider it all. It's such a new idea for me and a completely unknown undertaking." And he was anxious to talk with Elisabeth about all this, but he kept that to himself. McClure and the other men said they understood and would allow him a few days to think about it. Then they laid out the monthly financial support they were willing to give. They wanted him and Elisabeth to understand that all future Bushnell students would attend tuition free. Also, they proposed getting the school going right after Christmas.

After the men left, James learned that Elisabeth wasn't as surprised as her husband. She knew how people liked James and respected his positive and enthusiastic attitude. And most of them knew he loved books and reading. In the couple's private discussion later that night, Elisabeth reminded him about all his visits to the library back in Hannibal, Missouri. That was where they'd first met. Smiling together warmly, they reminisced about their secret meetings at that library. She pointed out that even as an 18-year-old working on the Mississippi wharf, James had spent as much time as he could borrowing and reading a variety of books. And now, adding to that, James had proven himself an extremely trustworthy and hard worker to all his new neighbors and acquaintances.

James thought deeply about what the school would mean to the little Grand Prairie community growing up all around them. Always responding well to a challenge, he agreed to give it a try. His first step was to borrow a few Bibles and other books from friends and relatives. Books were few and precious among the settlers and James promised to guard them with his life if necessary! He then worked up the nerve to ask Isaac and Elias Briggs to donate and order twenty slates and four dozen chalk sticks, by convincing them that they were fostering the future of Lane County. Being generous men and supportive, Elias and Isaac gladly obliged. Unfortunately, it took James' anticipated writing supplies a full three months to travel from Fort Vancouver to Oregon City and to finally arrive in Salem. School was almost out for the Spring by the time James drove to Salem to get their new slates and boxes of chalk.

The schoolchildren met in an old log cabin 15 feet square in all and 7 feet up to the ceiling poles. It was heated by a large dirt fireplace on one side that smoked fearfully upon occasion. Twenty-two lively students gathered on split log benches above the dirt floor. All the students were above age ten except one younger boy and one little girl. Like James, these students didn't have much, if any, experience with formal schooling. For the first few days, James strived just to keep order. One of the oldest boys, Frank, stood up from his desk often and stretched his long arms in the air. He regularly complained loudly things like, "I'm going to be a farmer like my dad. I don't know why I need to learn this history stuff!" Or another of his frequent complaints, "I am too old for schooling. I shouldn't be here."

Another lad, Thomas, always tried to get everyone to laugh at his silliness. He'd use his pencil to poke whoever had the misfortune to sit in front of him and always snickered until all his chums around him were watching to see what was going to happen. The boys loved it when the poking victim got mad or annoyed and laughed louder and louder. Unfortunately, most of the class was easily stirred up and distracted.

Demanding as it was, James didn't back down from his work. He was determined to give these youth a common school education and drill proper study habits into his unruly and boisterous students. He shared all his problems with Elisabeth and the couple prayed together many times that first week.

Attempting to begin better classroom order after the first frustrating week, James decided his students needed assigned seats. He spent one whole evening thinking over a good seating chart to put in use. He set the oldest boy, Frank, next to the youngest lad, Billy, and would make him a tutor for the little one. Billy was the little brother to one of Frank's best pals. Hopefully, that would keep Frank busier and prevent some of the daily turmoil the lanky youth enjoyed causing.

Then, he separated the boys from the girls, too. The four oldest girls were a big distraction for the older boys, who were constantly trying to get their attention. By assigning those four girls to each help a younger girl, or possibly even two, he hoped would give the young misses some confidence. Also, he was fairly sure they would thoroughly learn the content themselves as they taught it to the smaller girls.

James felt inspired and more confident, as he liked these new ideas. Now, if only his students would, too!

After opening with prayer on Monday morning, James announced that students would no longer choose their own seats. As expected, this was met by a lot of groans and muttering. Nevertheless, he ignored them and directed all the students into two groups with girls to his left and boys to his right. He'd previously moved the benches farther apart to widen the center aisle. After the girls started moving, the boys were forced to get moving also. Then he assigned two older and two younger children to spots on the same bench and repeated this until all students had a spot in the new arrangement. Frank, who'd grumbled the loudest, even to the point of disrespect, quieted down when he was assigned to help his pal Joe's little brother. Frank spoke gruffly, but once he turned his back on his peers and faced the younger boy, Billy, James noticed Frank softened his tone quite a bit. Soon it was apparent that Frank liked being in charge and ordering Billy about. James thought and hoped that Billy could handle it.

By noon that day, James was seeing some positive change as most of the older students rose to the challenge of helping. He smiled and sent a silent grateful prayer upwards.

This winter was proving to be exceptionally cold once again, with deep snow on the ground. One Monday morning in late January, they all awoke to new snow and more ice covering over the previously frozen layers. Deciding to leave his horse at home in its warm barn and not make the poor beast have to stand outside all day, James told Elisabeth he was going to walk to school. James dressed extra warmly and thanked Elisabeth with a kiss for the warm woolen mittens she'd given him recently at Christmas. After breakfast, he started slowly trudging through the snow to school, working hard to keep his balance. He held the precious borrowed books in a canvas bag hooked over one arm, which didn't help his balance. Mittens and all, he'd also wished he could blow some added warmth into them.

He made it to school in one piece without any bad falls or books ending up in the snow. Still, it took him much longer than the ordinary 15–20 minutes. He worried about being late getting school started. Once at the schoolhouse door, he found he had to push away a two-foot pile of snow to even get the door to swing open. Pulling strenuously, he finally got it open. He found the building full of snow, but empty of scholars. Now what should he do about the snow? He built a fire and paced the aisle back and forth, waiting for the building to warm up. No student ever appeared that morning. After several hours of waiting, James scratched on a board "School closed today."

It turned out that school was postponed for the rest of the week as the temperatures stayed below zero.

# CHAPTER ELEVEN

## Starting a Church and Building a School

ONE SUNDAY IN MARCH, James, and his family, including his mother, were all visiting at sister Helen's. Stretching out on Helen's colorful rag rug with baby Jennette sitting on his stomach, James groaned aloud. "That was such a delicious meal, Helen. I'm as full as a tick and ready to pop. This afternoon makes me think back to those great Sunday potlucks after church in Kirksville. Weren't those good times? I'm missing that here today, aren't you? I miss the fellowship of other Christian families and the opportunities to worship together with them. And, I reckon, it's not only our family missing this, but many of our neighbors, too. We certainly can't be the only ones missing a church."

Helen replied slowly, as in thought. "First, I'm very glad you enjoyed the meal, James. It's nice to have some company in our home. And, next, you're right. Mrs. Callison was just talking like you are now, when she came to call Monday. She was mentioning missing a church and all that goes with it. It does make me wonder who else is feeling this way."

Helen paused, then continued, "Well, maybe, Edward and I could host a Sunday gathering to discuss starting a new church and see who comes. After that, we'll just see what happens. We can leave it all up to God, I'm sure. Help me spread the word, you three."

Elisabeth caught the vision, "Oh, how exciting! To think we may soon get to have church again!"

And that was how their simple church meetings began in the Grand Prairie community. They met first in the Adkins' home, but soon moved into the Bryant's larger house. Every Sunday, James, Elisabeth and his mother, the Adkins, the two McClure families, and several others gathered for fellowship, Bible reading and prayer. Two of the men played the fiddle and taking turns playing, they managed a few hymns. This special time soon became the highlight of James' and Elisabeth's week.

Then they could hardly contain their excitement when, in June of 1855, a preacher named Philip Mulkey started a circuit-riding ministry. He rode from his Eugene home into the surrounding communities. When Mulkey was in their area, he gladly agreed to preach in the Adkins home. His Bible teaching was a thrilling dose of spiritual energy to the Bushnell, Adkins, and McClure families, as well as all the others who attended.

Pastor Philip Mulkey also preached in two other communities and eventually three new churches were started. On the fourth Sunday in June 1885, Mulkey gladly accepted the Grand Prairie Church's call to pastor. Their church became the First Christian Church at Clear Lake with 14 members. Another church elder, Gilmore Callison, also preached occasionally in their new church. Within the first months, James and Elisabeth eagerly became official church members. They each made a confession of their faith and Elisabeth was baptized by immersion in the lake. For James, who'd been baptized in the Mississippi River as a young man working in Hannibal, this was a time of enthusiastic reaffirmation. It seemed natural that, within a month, James was selected as a deacon.

A year later, in the spring of 1856, the community decided to build a new schoolhouse at Grand Prairie. James and his students had spent one miserable year in the old log structure, so a new schoolhouse was very appealing. A grateful James was contracted to help with the new building, and he worked alongside a few of his friends.

His first assigned task was constructing the ceiling. With boards cut at Briggs' sawmill, James carefully hand-planed the dry planks as smoothly as he could get them. Finally, when he had the right number of planks dressed, he got to work mating, or joining two boards together to double the wood's thickness. Then, he was ready to place the joined boards in the ceiling frame with some new nails purchased for the school's construction. It was amazing to James that the nails were so shiny and went in so smoothly. He'd gotten used to the hand-forged, squarish nails and these were such a nice contrast. James was also contracted to put in the heating for the schoolhouse. Having some experiences with good and bad fireplaces, he was determined to build the best he could. He told Elias Briggs that he really wanted to put in a woodstove, but they were lacking the funds for that. "I guess I'm stuck with a fireplace, again. I really want to build one better than the one we had at that last old schoolhouse. It smoked terribly and often burned the children's eyes."

Elias stroked his beard slowly replied, "I've heard of a new design by a man called Rumford. John Powell was talking about it when he last came from back East. It seems that in order to improve the amount of heat going into the room and not so much up the chimney, the fireplace isn't built square. Instead, the back of the fireplace is built one third of the width of the front opening. Then the two sides angle from the front to the back side about 135 degrees. We should try it, James. I'd like to help you and see if it works."

With clay bricks and mortar, the two men did the best they could putting together the new fireplace on the south wall. When it was completed, they invited their families in for the inaugural fire. The two women and all their children shared in the excitement as they watched James use his flint and steel sparks to ignite the straw bedding. It caught quickly and soon the kindling was on fire and snapping heartily. It was only a few minutes before they could tell that the heat from the flames effectively drew in the smoke and pushed it up the chimney. James began slapping Elias on the back. "There's almost no smoke!" and the two men jumped around in a circle sending the children into giggles. Then, Elisabeth announced that she could actually feel the heat as it spread outwards more than ever before in her life. She started to laugh but didn't move away from the wonderful warmth she was feeling. Both she and Mary warmed their hands by the fire, even though it was the middle of August!

James and Elias were quite proud of their fireplace and enjoyed showing it off to one and all for the next several months. After all the school's construction work was completed, there was still no rest for James. He was asked to teach the first class of students that Fall. The new building became a gathering place for the surrounding county and put to a variety of public uses.

At the end of another year, the First Christian Church meetings moved from the Adkins' home to the new Grand Prairie Schoolhouse on Meadow View Road. It became officially known as The Grand Prairie Church on November 28, 1858. It remained a strong church in the community until it reorganized into the Junction City Christian Church and the Alvadore Christian Church much later.

The Alvadore Christian Church 1890

James also began building a better and bigger house for his own family that fall. They moved into their third home in December of 1856. On September 1, 1857, the Bushnells' second daughter was born, Ursula Josephine. Charles and, especially three-year-old Nettie, were delighted to have a baby sister. Then, two years later on October 9, 1859, Mary Elisabeth was born. This baby girl only stayed on Earth with them for a brief two weeks. They buried her on a Sunday with a small group of their church friends and family present. That very same night, Josephine became sick with erysipelas, an infected rash on her little legs and feet. The doctor was called in from Eugene. With breaking hearts, Elisabeth and James watched as their dear two-year-old Josephine suffered on for weeks. The doctor had rendered a bad diagnosis and treatment. Her little body finally grew too weary, and she died on November third. She had been such a bright, beautiful, and loving little girl, that James grieved like he had never grieved before. He had now lost two little ones within the same month. His sister Helen heard James say to Edward many months later, "This is the greatest trial of my life. I would have gladly gone up with either of them if it had been God's will."

Both Elisabeth and Helen completely understood James' grief, but they were dumbfounded at the many months he remained so deeply grief-stricken. Even Elisabeth didn't know how to console him. It certainly helped all their spirits when she soon became pregnant again.

As February came along that year, so did statehood to the Oregon Territory. Oregon was now separate from Washington and California and had become the 33rd state in the nation. A group of settlers representing both Canadian interests and Oregon settlements had met at Champoeg throughout the 1840s to determine the state's future. Boundaries were agreed upon and votes were taken. A provisional government was established first. Then on February 14, 1859, Oregon's statehood became official. Each town held a celebration. Junction City invited the outlying communities into its town square. There was music, food, and the clamor of gunshots mingled with happier sounds. A feeling of pride hung in the air almost as thick as the foggy weather around them. The crazy behaviors of the adults made for a sight that Charles and Nettie would never forget!

# CHAPTER TWELVE

## *Time to fence the farm*

ON JULY 10, 1860, James and Elisabeth were blessed with a new baby boy. They named him William Francis. Charles Alvah was now nine years old, and Lucy Jennette was six. They all desperately prayed for this little one to stay healthy and alive.

After enjoying their new home for five years, James and Elisabeth had made most of their planned improvements. Their huge barn was secure, too. To James way of thinking, the only problem now was the marauding bands of wild horses and Spanish cattle that roamed wherever they pleased. All that winter, these cows, with their long sharp horns and their half-wild ways, terrorized folks in the local area. He really needed to get his fencing up, especially now that he'd seen two of those unwelcome cattle hanging around their barn a few times in the past couple of weeks. Although they seemed more of a nuisance than anything else to him, he still warned his family: "If you see any, stay away from them and don't get to thinking they are friendly. They're not!"

His kids nodded their heads, acknowledging their father's orders. To everyone's relief, a week passed with no more signs of the pesky beasts.

Early one cloudy, wet morning, Elisabeth decided to go out to milk the cows before breakfast. She wanted to enjoy some cream in her coffee, and she'd used up yesterday's supply baking biscuits and flapjacks. She took James' heavy coat and hat off the chair where he'd hung them to dry overnight. She quietly opened and closed the door, hoping the others could keep sleeping. Yawning as she walked to their newly enlarged barn, she reached out and grabbed the smooth door handle. Some movement caught her eye to her right, however, and she stopped dead in her tracks. Turning just her head, she found herself staring eye to eye with a wild longhorn just a few yards away. Then, as she stood frozen and terrified, he went from simply staring with his menacing black eyes, to lowering his head, snorting and pawing the ground. Elisabeth didn't take her eyes off him. Knowing she had to do something before he charged at her, she started slowly raising the door latch, keeping the rest of her body motionless. With her heart pounding like a drum, she took a slow, long breath, then pulled the barn door open as swiftly as she could, swept inside, and yanked the door closed behind her.

She took a moment to breathe, settle her nerves and slow her racing heart. Now, she realized, she was stuck in the barn with that mean cow or bull or whatever it was, waiting outside the door for her! But for the moment she was safe. She quietly and slowly eased over to her cows. She stroked Emmy's back first. "Did you hear that, ol' girl? There's an unfriendly relative of yours out there. He's on your Spanish side of the family and he's up to no good."

Giving a final pat to Emmy, she went ahead and readied the bucket and the stool for milking. "I might as well get my chores done while I'm in here. I'll deal with that other critter again when I must."

Elisabeth calmed herself down as she first milked Emmy and then, feeling sorry for the uncomfortable Bessy, went ahead and milked her, too. It wasn't like she was anxious to leave the barn anytime soon. When the bucket was full there was nothing else left for her to do in the barn. "Surely," she thought, "James will be up and around soon." But since she wasn't sure when, she began to bang on the door with a shovel and yell as loud as she could.

"James! James! Help me! I'm stuck in the barn. Help!" she yelled repeatedly. She finally heard the cabin door open and shut and at last heard her husband yelling back, "What do you mean you're stuck? Is it the door?"

"There's a mean Spanish cow out there!" she gasped and then yelled. "Be careful! He was just there when I came out to milk."

"Ohhhh," James replied as he slowed his pace and carefully looked all around him. "Well, I think he's cleared out now." He swung open the barndoor and took the bucket from his wife. He set it on the ground and hugged her. She rested in his arms and in a muffled voice said, "That beast went from staring to ready to charge me so fast I wasn't sure I'd make it into the barn soon enough. Thank the good Lord, I did."

"I'm sorry for your scare this morning, Lizzie. Perhaps for a while I'd better go outside first in the morning and check out the yard."

"I won't argue with you," she answered. "So, the next time I want some cream for my coffee, I'll just send you out to get it. Right?"

"It's a deal," he said chuckling and giving her a warm smile.

One sunny June morning in 1861, James found Elisabeth and baby Willie in the kitchen. He grabbed his tin cup from its peg on the wall and reached for the coffee percolating on their new cast iron stove. Pouring the steaming brown liquid, he said, "I think it's a fine day to start that fencing project I've been ruminating about. The posts and lumber are dried out as much as they'll ever get in this weather. You know, if I wait for them to dry completely, the fence will never get built. Lizzie, do you care if I start it now? It will keep me outside and busy most of the summer days ahead."

Elisabeth turned from the stove and grinned slyly, saying, "That has some advantages and disadvantages. Nettie has become an immense help with the baby. And I think Charles is old enough to be of help to you, don't you think? Given that, I think we girls can manage in the house here while you two work outside there."

James grinned and winked at his daughter as she entered the kitchen. "Nettie, did you hear that compliment from your Ma? You've grown into a good little helper now." The little girl looked at her mother in a sleepy stupor and said "Really? Does that mean I'm old enough to learn to sew now, Ma? I really want to learn how to make clothes, not just watch Willie all the time and help with the cleaning. I already know how to do all that."

Afraid of where this conversation was going, Elisabeth quickly answered with "When I have the time to teach you, but it won't happen this summer, Jennette. There are too many other chores needing doing in the summertime."

James, turning to avoid Nettie's appealing eyes, said, "I'm leaving you two women to go out and feed the stock. I'll be back in an hour for breakfast," and hurried out the door. It was just too easy for him to give in to his daughter and that often got him in trouble with Elisabeth.

James spent that summer fencing in some of his acres to hold his animals. He used the "stake and rider" style fence. He spent several days just splitting logs for the rails, or riders as they called them out west. Those riders were then hoisted and stacked up horizontally, one on top of the other. Young Charles usually worked with his father a good half day before starting to tire out. When James saw his son slowing down, he'd send him back to tend their garden along with Elisabeth and Nettie. Still, the 11-year-old boy was a big help and James finished fencing by Fall. Because they'd also managed to keep their crops watered and tended, they reaped all their Fall crops and had a bountiful harvest. Then, more good news came with the harvest. Elisabeth was pregnant again.

One night at supper, James shared some of his latest ideas. "Lizzie, what do you think about storing our wheat and oats in the barn during the winter? I know it's unusual, but we have the room, and it rains so much in this valley. This would keep it dry. Then again, I'd have to hire at least one more fella to help me haul it all inside. It's a thought that keeps coming to mind."

"Hmmm," she murmured. "If there's room and you have the energy, I don't see why it would hurt. It would keep the feed safe for our stock and away from those horrid Spanish cattle." After Elisabeth's reasoning was considered, they both agreed to the extra work they'd need to do. With hired help, their winter feed would be stored on the sheaves inside the barn.

They had a pleasant and mild fall. Elisabeth felt quite well in this pregnancy. They happily finished the month of September with no hint of what was to come.

# CHAPTER THIRTEEN

IN OCTOBER 1861, THE whole region experienced very unusual weather: a series of early snowfalls, often leaving more than a foot on the valley floor and more in the Cascade Mountains. And then an early freeze. It turned so cold that some rivers that had never, ever been frozen did so that month. When the warmer weather finally returned, most people breathed a sigh of relief, happy to have those freezing conditions behind them.

But on November 1st it commenced raining—and it continued to rain or snow every single day of the long, cold, and dreary month. The surrounding hills and mountains had been brilliant and sparkling white by the first of December. But that beauty was short-lived when suddenly the weather turned warm. Heavy rains continued to fall day after day. Eventually the rain melted the snow and ice on the hills and that run-off headed toward the river and low-lying lands with an angry current. The ground was already fully saturated and couldn't absorb any more water. This rapid snow melt caused the rivers to rise quickly. Soon the floodwaters from the Willamette River and its tributaries covered nearly the entire Willamette Valley.

Although the Bushnells had purposely selected their property's highest spot for their home site, the flood around their house rose to 14 inches above the ground. A few days later, James measured it at 18 inches deep. Most farmhouses had no basements or foundations to raise the houses above ground and the Bushnell home was no different. Elisabeth and Nettie worked hard to keep the first muddy waters out of the house with constant sweeping with the broom and frequent mopping, while also plugging the cracks with rolled towels, rugs and even bedding around the door and lower walls. James and Charles worked outside, industriously digging ditches to try to direct the river's flow away from the house. Finally getting most of the water draining away from the cabin, they went to work on their barn. That was a much bigger project.

First, they dragged hay bales over to line each of the inner walls. James murmured aloud to Charles, "I sure hope this barrier works to prevent the water from coming inside. I've got our entire harvest stored inside here and we certainly will need to feed our animals from it for the rest of the winter."

Then they moved their horses and cows from outside to the center of the barn. James decided they had to tie them to whatever they could find and not let them move freely. He didn't know what to expect, but knew his animals could get rambunctious, even dangerous, if frightened.

On the second day of flooding, James watched forlornly as nearly all his newly constructed fence was carried away in the current cutting swiftly across his fields. Being dry and light, his fence rails were quickly gone! Early the next morning while glumly checking his flooded land from inside their one and only front room glass window, James noticed a great many unfamiliar fence rails floating down towards him from up above his farm. He dashed outside through the water and watched as some of these new floating slabs got lodged on their higher grounds. He ran back and yelled inside to Charles, who quickly put on his boots. They each grabbed their heaviest coats, and both ran out to that hillside. Sloshing through the water, between the two of them they captured all those floating rails and dragged them into their barn. They worked all day. It took many trips because the runaway rails just kept traveling towards them downstream with the current. Before nightfall, Charles and James had collected quite a few piles to air out the best they possibly could inside their mostly dry barn.

Using these newly stockpiled slabs, James started rebuilding right after the floods receded. He and Charles worked steadily every day to re-fence most of their wheat fields and got them completely fenced within that week. Then they sorely wished they could take a day to relax from their strenuous refencing project, but instead they had to tackle some minor damage to the house and barn.

It was Sunday the eighth of December and their small church still gathered to worship, even with the high water all around. While they were singing hymns that morning, the floodwaters quickly rose and reclaimed the ravaged lands once more. The Bushnells and their neighbors could scarcely believe the difference in the high water before and after church. It shocked them to realize that this time the flood was higher than they'd ever seen before! James drove them home from church as quickly as the team could navigate the mud and deep waters. When they arrived home, they found their newest fence had completely fallen and was folded up all together like a fan. Then, while the family stopped and were all staring wide-eyed, they watched sorrowfully as the fence was completely picked up by the floodwater and carried off downstream to some unknown destination.

James shook his head. He couldn't believe he was left in the same fix as the week before when the first flood had hit them. Having just been to church, Elisabeth reminded the family that God promised "to walk with them through the floods" and "they would not be overcome." James quickly affirmed that he'd always put his faith to work believing those very promises. They each tried not to be discouraged by these troubles, as hard as they seemed.

The last of the water had scarcely left their area when it turned bitterly cold. It seemed like all at once Winter had turned her icy breath upon them. The grass and all that had been under water was still completely covered with sand and mud. Everywhere was a filthy mess and now it was a frosty, filthy mess.

However, their biggest problems came with the next rain. Once again, it rained for weeks and weeks on end, through Christmas and the whole of January. Many people lost their barns, crops, animals and even homes in the relentless floods. Farther north in the valley, towns and warehouses were wiped out. James heard that towns he'd visited such as Champoeg and Canemah, up near Oregon City, were completely washed away. Their buildings, trees, and dead animals were found all the way up to Astoria and then carried out to the sea. Because bridges were down in many places, merchandise transport halted, much business was stopped, and countless businesses ruined. Many schools couldn't open for months.

As if more high water wasn't enough, a heavy snowfall followed the flood disaster, leaving a layer of sleet covering the ground until March. Every single blade of grass or twig carried a heavy coat of ice. The trees in the nearest oak grove were laden with sparkling ice. But this glistening beauty came with the terrifying sounds of limbs cracking and eventually crashing to the ground. These disturbing sounds were frightening to Elisabeth and the children at first. However, they soon realized they were in no danger from trees that were far away, and they became more accustomed to the noises.

During this long, wet and bitter winter, the half wild Spanish cattle roamed the ice-covered prairies and were forced to paw through 12 to 16 inches of snow to find a morsel to eat. The cattle soon starved to death. The wild horses lasted longer, but James saw only two that survived.

As far as any old-timer knew, this was the worst winter ever experienced in the Willamette Valley. Even with it being one of the coldest winters ever known, the memory of the relentless floods stood out the most. That year they saw rivers flood that had never flooded before. Afterwards, the settlers referred to it as "Noah's flood." Certainly, they had lived through the worst floods ever known in the state and 1861 became a year that all the Oregon families talked about for as long as they lived.

But it did come with some brighter spots. One was the birth of their sweet baby girl Helen Virginia. They named her after James' sister Helen, and Virginia was reminiscent of Elisabeth's childhood home back east.

Then in a completely unexpected way, that strange and cruel winter favorably altered James and Elisabeth's lives. It turned out to be very prudent when James had built a good sturdy barn and had quickly repaired any leaks and damage. And because he'd stored last summer's feed crops inside his barn, he now had plenty of feed for his animals. Because of that decision and the extra work it had taken, his dry feed proved enough to not only save his own stock but help a good many neighbors as well. Before Spring ended, the going price for a dozen sheaves was at the high cost of $1.00 for wheat and $1.50 for oats. Being one of the few farmers with any suitable feed in the whole region, James soon found people coming from near and far to buy from him. James' stroke of forethought, or 'Providential Guidance' as Elisabeth claimed, started the Bushnells on the most financially secure path they'd ever traveled.

Even though they'd survived the harsh winter in fine fettle, they discovered too late that much of their livestock had eaten a poisonous root that had stolen a ride on the early winter floods and settled in their grazing fields. It was yet another trial during their severely trying winter and spring seasons. As James looked hopefully towards the upcoming summer, he knew that fencing the farm would be high on the agenda—again!

# CHAPTER FOURTEEN

## The Civil War Reaches the West

THE NORTHEASTERN AND SOUTHERN states were experiencing bitter strife as a civil war was fiercely raging. Out west, the new settlers were experiencing it, too, but to lesser degrees. Most folks, including James and Elisabeth, hung a Liberty Pole near their front door to show where their loyalties stood and kept that starry banner flying. James' childhood and roots were in the North. When a company of cavalry was organized, James was chosen as first sergeant. James and his men went to summer camp at Salem in 1864 where the state held competitions. James' company won the prize for the "Best Drilled" and the "Finest Equipped" cavalry in the state. Fortunately, no fighting was ever necessary for his company.

Raised on a Virginia plantation, Elisabeth was more conflicted by the strife. Mostly, she worried about the safety of her family back home, since all but her brother Jason still lived in Virginia. Both she and James hated hearing the news of all the fighting and dying happening back east. Elisabeth could get very distressed worrying about her parents' farm being taken over by soldiers or destroyed in the battles she heard about. She loved the plantation and her memories of being raised there. Yet, being from the South put her in the minority out here in Oregon, so Elisabeth kept her qualms to herself and expressed her anxieties only to James. She was especially careful after the sad morning of April 14, 1865, when the news came of the assassination of President Lincoln. A bitter vengeful spirit was aroused in the breasts of the Union men. Any who dared to speak a word in favor of the rebels or a word against the President, put his or her life in danger.

Christians and their churches were put in a sensitive position as the war threatened their unity. Most of them were careful not to let it become divisive in their fellowships. Not so in the Christian Church of Grand

Prairie, though. It was split in two by the war. One prominent Elder held Confederate views, coming from the South before moving to Oregon. And so did all his children and some of his friends. This large group of southern sympathizers left the church in one bold move. The Elder's son hung a Confederate flag on his porch and rode around the communities shouting racial slurs. He was jailed for this and, for his own safety, had to be sent all the way to the Fort Vancouver barracks across the Columbia River. His father was heard to declare, "If I were still in Missouri, I'd take a gun and help shoot down the abolitionists." He never landed in jail as his son did, though.

Despite the tensions, James, as the head Elder, was able to steer his Grand Prairie Christian Church to the Bible's teaching of equality among all men and women. He gathered most of the church members into a formal stand against slavery. They also had weekly prayer meetings asking God to unite their divided country.

## AFTER THE WAR

In the spring of 1865, the Bushnell's dear little four-year-old Willie was called away to a better world. He was sick but for a brief time with pleurisy and nothing they could do seemed to help. As this was their third child lost to death in the past five years, they were emotionally devasted. Elisabeth, especially, appeared to have aged. Her movements were obviously weaker and slower as she had cared for Willie day in and day out. To get away from all their sorrow, James and Elisabeth, with their remaining three children, joined a group from their church going to Yaquina Bay. They planned to celebrate the Fourth of July in good old-fashioned style.

It was definitely still Indian country around the coastal bay. It didn't take Charles, Nettie, and Helen long to notice that there were no other non-Indian people in sight, outside their church group. On the Fourth, Elder Gilmore Callison delivered the oration. After that, Captain Kellogg, who ran the steamer on Yaquina Bay, gave a good talk. Everyone helped spread their dinner on a huge cedar log that had washed up on the sand. When they were done feasting, they shared their leftovers with the Indians who seemed to thoroughly enjoy the scraps.

In the fall of 1865, James bought three donation land claims from the Thomas Judson family— 800 acres for $4,000. He rented their former land on Grand Prairie to his brother-in-law, Jason Adkins. To Elisabeth's great joy, her brother had just arrived in Oregon that summer. Jason caught them up with all the latest news about the family plantation back home. He described the tremendous financial troubles caused by the war and how the farmers were struggling to exist and desperately hoping to rebuild. Jason thought the rebuilding of war savaged Virginia farms was going to take too long so he left the South to seek better prospects in Oregon.

Elisabeth, James, and their children moved back into the Bushnells' very first house. This structure was 13 years old and now had a shed to hold a wagon and their winter wood stacks. While living there, James built another house for his family in the winter of 1866, across the road from their old log cabin. This new one was a small, box style home that wasn't much to look at, but it was clean and light. It was a vast improvement over the older house they moved out from; that old one had neither been easily kept clean nor filled with very much light. Elisabeth gave birth to baby George Addison in their new house that winter. After all their building and moving, and now having a new baby to care for, Elisabeth was happy to get settled into a more permanent home. She wasn't such a doer and mover, like her husband.

That was the same year that James' oldest brother, George, arrived from Missouri. A year ago, George and his large family first went to Sonoma County, California, but soon headed north to join the rest of the Bushnells. George's move made a total of six members from James' family all residing in Oregon now. The exception was William, who had moved back to San Francisco.

# CHAPTER FIFTEEN

*Elvan M. Pitney, his 10th birthday*

## AUGUST 6, 1934

ELVAN HAD BEEN THINKING about his birthday wishes. No one had asked him, but he just couldn't help it. He was going to blow out all the candles on his cake after dinner and had been busy making up wishes all afternoon. Later that night, he'd have to decide on just one wish as that was the tradition in his family. He'd been told only one birthday wish would come true.

After he'd delivered a cold lunch to his father and 14-year-old-brother working out in the hay field, he started daydreaming again while walking the dusty, dirt lane back to the house. Once inside and washed up, he sat down to the noon meal with his tall mother and tiny grandmother. He waited until after Mom said the blessing. Then, he just blurted out, "Grandma, did you ever get to go see the ocean?"

His grandmother looked at his mother with amused surprise. Then, she slowly unfolded her napkin and turned to him. "Yes, the first time I got to see the ocean I was right about your age."

She went on. "It was after a very sad time Elvan, when my two little sisters had died, and then five-year-old Willie Francis died. Did you know that's who your Uncle Francis is named after? My little brother William Francis?"

Elvan just nodded silently as he chewed his bread and jam.

"Papa and Mama tried to cheer us all up with a trip to the beach for the 4th of July celebration. Our family joined a church group going to Yaquina Bay, a big bay that has a nice river running into it before it enters the Pacific Ocean. Papa drove our wagon with Mama beside him and we three children rode in the back. We all got to sit right on top of our camping gear. It was very bumpy up there, but more fun for us though. We stopped when we got to the open bay. The smooth water was lined with big hills covered by tall evergreen trees on one side and a long sandy beach along the opposite side. We headed to the ocean, and I was so excited when Papa said we'd set up camp on a small bluff looking right over the beach, right where the bay ran into the ocean.

"I noticed how gray the beach was, and the water was gray and even the sky was gray! Everyone's mood was bright, though. At least brighter than it had been. I still remember how exciting it was to go to sleep that night hearing the crash of the ocean waves rolling nearby. The next day was the Fourth. The adults let us children play in the sand and run in the waves while they had a church service. The day was a little cool and the water was very cold. Still, Charles, Helen and I just let our feet and legs get numb in the water until we couldn't feel the cold and then really enjoyed playing in the ocean. We would run to the family campfire to warm up and then back out we'd go—just to get cold and wet all over again!

"After the adults finished hearing Elder Callison preach, I decided to join in and listen. I sat next to River Captain Kellogg. He looked interesting and he ran a steamer ship on the bay. He spoke next, and it was fascinating for me to hear about his life on the river. He'd led such an exciting life— spending lots of time both on the river and on the ocean! He talked about all the fish and animals he had seen and, Elvan, I was just about green with envy.

"Then the day only got more interesting. All the food was spread out like a huge feast on an immense log that had washed up on the beach. I remember thinking it was so clever that we could use the log for a banquet table. Then to my amazement, Indians started appearing through the trees from the wooded hills around us! They came in what looked to me like family groups. The groups stopped and gathered silently all around us. Captain Kellogg greeted them with hand signals and spoke aloud in English, too. He then asked Elder Callison to go ahead and ask God to bless our meal. When I looked up after the prayer, I saw the Indians still watching us. It was hard for me not to stare at them, but Mama said we children shouldn't stare. I'd only seen one other Indian before this, so you can imagine how much I wanted to watch them. The one I'd seen before was a woman from the Kalapuya tribe and she looked a little different from these Alsi people, who were shorter and quieter. We began eating and the Indians still just stood silently watching us. When our group had finished all the food we could eat, Papa and the other men motioned to the Indians, inviting them to come and clean up the rest of it. So, we switched places with the Indians and all of us just really stared outright—children and grownups alike—we couldn't help it. We watched as the Indians quickly ate every little bit we'd left, chicken bones and all! Nothing was left when they got done but the empty platters. Our womenfolk grabbed those up quickly just in case the Indians thought they could have them, too.

"We camped one more night there on the bank of that bay and, again, I enjoyed the roar of the ocean. But the thought of all those Indians so close around us made me nervous. I didn't sleep well, and I know Helen didn't either because she wiggled all night long and stayed very close beside me. We packed up the next morning and had to say goodbye to the ocean. That was sad for me. It was many years before I got to go back to the seaside."

Elvan's mom had been listening quietly to Grandmother's story, also. She must have already guessed where his questions had originated. His grandmother probably did, too. His mom asked then, "Do you remember the week we spent together in Yachats when you were younger, Elvan? That was very close to Yaquina Bay."

"Yes, Mama, I do. I really loved it there. I'm wishing we could go again, now that I'm older. "

And with that, Mother and Grandmother just quietly smiled at each other and kept on eating.

In just another moment, though, his grandmother said, "Elvan, as soon as I'm done eating, come with me and we'll get out my shell collection. It's stored in my trunk, and I haven't looked it over in a while."

**Lucy Jennette Bushnell with grandson Elvan**

# CHAPTER SIXTEEN

## *James and Elisabeth*

### SPRING 1867

WHEN BABY ADDISON, OR Addie as they called him, was five months old, James approached Elisabeth in the kitchen one early spring day, "We're goin' be short a few farmhands this month. The Haughman boys are both still recovering from pleurisy so I'm trying to think of who else we can find to help us get our crops set in. I'm counting on Charles and Nettie, some, to help me this year. Can you think of any other hirable men, Lizzie? Maybe we could hire one of Charles' friends to come for a month?" James stroked his beard and stopped talking, still deep in thought.

Elisabeth had been mixing up some yellow cornmeal dough when James had started talking to her. She kept slowly stirring the lumpy dough with the wooden spoon with one hand and firmly holding the crockery with the other. She looked at James pensively, "Well, here's a thought. What if I put Nettie to work in the house and then I'd be free to help you get the crops planted. I know how to work hard. You'd be taking a chance with a young fellow we've hardly met. Some of them know how to work and some of them just don't. Nettie is old enough to care for the babies, the housework and do some of the cooking. We can wait to plant the garden if need be."

She put down the bowl and faced him directly. "After this dreary winter and all the household goings-on, I think I'd like a chance to get outside. The change of scenery and fresh air sounds nice. And, you know," she said grinning now, "You wouldn't have to pay me. We could save that money instead."

So, they agreed to try Elisabeth's plan. She asked for two days to get Nettie trained in the household routine and tasks. Nettie was agreeable and anxious to prove she could do what it took to run the house. "I am almost 14 now, you know," she reminded her mother more than once. Charles and James had already gotten one field plowed. It was a cool, but sunny morning in late April when Elisabeth set outside to work. Going to the freshly tilled field, she began dropping her seed corn in the muddy burrows. She sang or hummed as she plodded along. She stopped at the end of each row to stretch and look around, then she'd start down the next furrow. Most sunny days, Nettie walked out to visit with the baby in her arms and little Helen in tow. Sometimes five-year-old Helen was left to "help" her mother and play in the field up until noontime. And sometimes Charles worked with Elisabeth, too. Charles always preferred using their rolling corn seeder. Elisabeth had always preferred the hand scattering method to start with and kept that up as long as she could. Though, once James had more fields prepared, she didn't want to get behind and began sowing using the rolling iron seeder, too. It helped speed up her progress a bit.

When the corn was planted and she started in the grain fields, she did broadcast seeding again as fast as she could. Her self-proclaimed goal was to not fall more than two fields behind the horse and plow. With Charles helping, they usually could get to the next freshly plowed field not long after James finished preparing it.

Each day Elisabeth would quit about an hour earlier than the two men and head back to the house. Her routine from the first day on became: pull off her muddy boots outside the back door, open the door and ask Nettie to hand her the clean skirt set nearby. Then, still outside, she would shed the muddy skirt and slip into the clean one. Only then would she enter the house. Next, she washed her hands in the soapy water bucket Nettie had prepared by the door. Then, without any mud clinging to her from the fields, she hugged her little Helen and then the baby. While she nursed baby Addie, she chatted with Helen and Nettie about their day. After putting on clean shoes, she was ready to help Nettie get supper on the table. Nettie seemed to move into her new responsibilities quite easily. She only complained during the few days when the baby was teething and very fussy. Elisabeth knew that keeping the five-year-old out of trouble was a challenging task, but rarely heard any comments about it from Jennette. It certainly did help that little Helen was allowed to "help" out in the fields a few hours every day.

With this pleasant routine, they got five of their fields planted with oats and corn before the rain started up. It was disappointing that once the rain started, it didn't slack off for a whole week. The first two rainy days, James and Charles worked in the barn oiling harnesses and cleaning up the messy areas. Elisabeth stayed inside and got caught up with the washing, although she and Nettie had to hang it indoors. Elisabeth took most of it over to their old house across the lane to hang inside there— out of the way.

On the evening of the second night, with only dark clouds and more rain in sight, James announced, "This dinner is as good as I could get anywhere and better than most. You've been doing a really fine job cooking and cleaning, Lucy Jennette. I'm feeling so well taken care of that I'm ready to go back to the fields— even if it doesn't quit raining. Charles, I want you up and ready to go in the morning, too. So, dress as warmly as you can and be ready as soon as it's daylight, son. And be sure to get a good night's sleep tonight."

Because he hadn't addressed her, Elisabeth felt like James didn't expect her to help outdoors tomorrow. She started clearing up the plates and tin cups. As she dropped them in the warm water simmering on the stovetop, she said, "I'm going to go out tomorrow, too. You need the help and I'm not afraid of the rain. I've lived with it as long as you have, James. I've done about all I can do in here and not get in Nettie's way." She smiled proudly at her daughter and winked.

"I don't know. . ." James started to object but was cut off by Elisabeth walking over and standing directly in front of him.

"I can still put seeds into the soil, rain or no rain. It's not that cold anymore, just wet. I'm all set to help you, and I don't want you to argue with me!"

"Well, if you agree to come in somewhat earlier than you did last week, I'll take your help. You're a good worker, but I don't want to tire out the best wife I have. Oops! I meant the best wife in this county and the mother of my children!" he quickly corrected with a wink and a grin. "Mothering is an important job, too."

The two men went out to the fields early the next morning. Elisabeth had let James talk her into going out a little later and giving the morning weather a bit longer to warm up. So, she followed the men out after all the breakfast dishes and cleaning up was finished. She started sowing oats and did the best she could to keep herself warm and dry in the dampness, all but her hands and fingertips. At noon, they all stopped for the cold lunch that Nettie brought to them in the shed, where they'd decided to eat so they didn't have to strip off their muddy layers to go inside the house. Nettie carried out the two little ones to avoid the mud and sat them up on hay bales beside their parents. Now free-handed, Nettie quickly turned back to fetch hot coffee for the cold workers.

Baby Addie and little Helen provided the entertainment while the rest of the family ate and waited for their hot drinks. The baby was propped up on a quilt and enjoyed all their attention. Helen talked with her family a bit, ate a few bites and began exploring her surroundings in the barn.

Nettie returned with the coffee pot and cups. After she poured a cup for her mother, they heard Elizabeth sigh, "Ahhh, it feels so good just to warm my hands around this steaming cup. Thank you, dear girl."

James watched Nettie beaming at her mother's comment.

The father and son went out soon after. Elisabeth nursed Addison and then turned him over to Nettie again with a peck on his brow. She hugged her five-year-old daughter who was begging to play in the barn a while longer. With her mother's approval, little Helen was allowed to play in the barn on her own until her nap time.

This became their regular pattern for the next four days. It was on the fifth rainy day that Elisabeth didn't perk up during or after the lunch break in the barn. Instead, she lamented, "I just can't get warm today! Even the coffee isn't thawing out my hands." She held out her blue hands for all to see. James wasn't surprised, though. "I'm sure the temperature has dropped today. Where has that sunny weather gone that we just had earlier? Well, that's late April for you around here. It gets you all excited about spring and then drops you back into winter."

He turned to Elisabeth and said, "If you don't get warmed up working this afternoon, Lizzie, I'd like you to go inside and find something to do in the house." He was prepared for her to argue with him and expected she'd remind him how he needed her help. Surprisingly, she replied, "I'll see how it goes. I just may do that." And she did. Within two hours, James watched her trudge back to the house. He noticed with some concern that she was moving very slowly. When James and Charles went in at the end of that day, Elisabeth was sitting by the stove peeling potatoes.

"Have you warmed up yet, Lizzie?" James asked as he hung his damp coat over a chair by the stove.

"Not completely," she murmured as she kept peeling. He noticed that she already had one full kettle of potatoes on the stove cooking.

Getting into their bed that night, James gladly held his wife close to him. She claimed she still wasn't warm and needed to 'borrow' his warmth. He just smiled. He didn't care if her feet were cold; she still felt very good, cozied right up next to him.

When he awoke the next morning though, she didn't stir. He quietly dressed and crept out to the kitchen, started the fire and began heating the kettle. Nettie came in next and started the eggs to boil. He smiled at his daughter and whispered that they should let her mother sleep a bit. James did go wake up Charles, though. And when the eggs and coffee were ready, James went in to raise Elisabeth, also.

"Breakfast is ready. Are you ready to get up?"

"Oh dear. Did I sleep that long? I'm getting up." And she did. Her voice revealed a congested head and nose, though. He watched her getting dressed and went out to the kitchen again. He was buttering his second piece of bread when Elisabeth appeared.

"Well, sounds to me like you've caught a cold, dear. How did you sleep?" he greeted her.

"I slept pretty well, but I didn't think I would ever warm up! Apparently, I did though, as I sure slept late this morning, didn't I?" she smiled. "I feel well enough that I can go out to work, now."

"Well . . ." he mused. "How about only until noontime and then we'll see how you're doing?"

Elisabeth nodded in agreement as she sipped her coffee. Both Charles and Nettie silently watched this exchange and didn't say a thing.

Out the three workers went into a drizzle quite common in the Willamette Valley. The sky and the landscape were all gray and wet. Overall, they were more than halfway finished planting fields and felt good about their progress. By noon, Elisabeth said she needed to go inside and trudged slowly towards the house. She was surprised how tired she felt and complained to James, when he met up with her on the way to the house, that her runny nose had been very irritating as she worked. She didn't mention being tired, however. Not until he said, "I can tell you're dragging now, Elisabeth. You're walking like you're all done in."

"Well, I suppose I can't deny it. I am tired." She smiled tentatively. "I think some food and a nice break will give me some pep again."

"We'll see," he smiled back at her.

After their noon break, Elisabeth insisted she felt better and was ready to go back out. She lasted almost as long as her usual afternoon time and then steered herself slowly back to the house. Instead of helping Nettie with supper chores, this day she sat reading to Helen by the fire and actually nodded off. When the men came in, she roused herself and got busy putting the supper on. She smiled bashfully at her eldest daughter as though she was ashamed about her nap.

Her coughing started during dinner. At first it seemed like she had just swallowed something wrong. But by bedtime, Elisabeth's cough unmistakably heralded a cold coming on. James encouraged her to go to bed early and forego her nightly mending. She started to mend some socks but only got one done and put her hands in her lap. "You're right, James. I'm tired enough to go to bed already."

That was the last day Elisabeth worked in the fields. Her cold worked its way from congestion in her nose and head into a worse cough within the week. Her congested coughing sounded terrible and was hard for her loved ones to listen to. She sent Nettie out to the fields to be substitute help in her place in the afternoons. When the baby slept, she would read to Helen in the afternoons some and rest with the little girl snuggled up close to her. But after two weeks of the cough, it was time to call the doctor in. Since the doctor said the cold had settled in her lungs, he recommended lots of warm tea with honey and directed them to turn the hot teakettle towards her face so she could inhale the steam. She was to do those three times a day sitting up in a chair. The rest of the time she was to rest in bed. He also promised a return visit in five days to see if she had improved any.

Elisabeth didn't improve. Her cough continued and it weakened her more and more. It was late in June when the doctor gravely told them Elisabeth had consumption or tuberculosis, as some called it. She was confined to her bed all that summer. As she grew weaker, she became helpless, not even able to nurse or hold the baby. James sent for his mother to come help. She tried helping with Elisabeth's care but ended up doing the cooking and laundry for the family, while also watching little Helen and the baby.

But it was young Nettie who ended up feeding her mother spoonful by spoonful two times a day. Other times it was Mother Bushnell who bathed, fed and comforted their patient. However, even with the loving care of the two women, young and old, in a few weeks James also had to start helping with Elisabeth's feeding as they could all see that his mother was worn out. James began regularly reading the Bible at Elisabeth's bedside each evening. The entire household was comforted by the soothing words and his strong voice reading God's promises aloud. They got through that summer with some hired help during the harvest. A few dear friends came over to help Nettie and Mother Bushnell preserve the summer fruits and vegetables. They missed Elisabeth cheery presence enormously. Nettie had become a substitute mother for the baby and little Helen, as well as a daily nurse for her mother. James was proud of how well their 14-year-old accepted her many tasks without complaining.

However, in the middle of September Elisabeth began refusing Mother Bushnell's or Nettie's help, and increasingly only allowed James to wait on her. She became quite anxious and clung to James like a little child, crying and petulant if he tried to leave. Weakly, and in barely a whisper at times, Elisabeth reminded James repeatedly about his promise— that he would never willingly leave her again. That was the promise he made to her back in 1854 after their 20-month separation, when they were freshly reunited and in search of their land claim. Each time she brought it up, James calmly reassured her that it was still true, and he wouldn't leave her.

Her extreme dependency on James went on for the next two months. He rarely got more than two hours of uninterrupted sleep. To get any relief at all, he had to sneak out while she napped. It was a demanding and exhausting duty, but he described to his mother that God sustained him and fulfilled His promise that "As thy day is, so shall thy strength be." Because of his inner strength and his own gift of good health, he was able to lovingly do all that he possibly could for Elisabeth. Even with all their devoted care, on January 2, 1868, she closed her eyes for the last time on Earth. She passed so quietly and gently that if James had not been watching her carefully at the precise time, he wouldn't have known that she'd left them. Spunky Elisabeth, who'd farmed alongside James and helped build homes and moved eight times in their marriage of 19 years, was finally resting in her permanent home.

# CHAPTER SEVENTEEN

IT WAS SNOWING FURIOUSLY the night Elisabeth died. And on January 4th, the day of her funeral, the snow was four inches deep and very wet. Then, to add to the family's sorrows, it suddenly turned very cold and quickly froze the wet ground. Then, it snowed again and kept snowing until it was 16 inches deep. Then the sleet came and covered everything with a glistening sheet of ice, reminiscent of the historic winter of 1861. Confined mostly inside now with the layers of ice everywhere outside, the Bushnells huddled together, absorbing their loss.

James now had four children to raise alone: Charles Alva, age 17; Lucy Jennette, age 14; Helen Virginia, age 6; and George Addison, age 3. The first two were quite old enough to keep in school, but the others were too young. In fact, as they were also too young to leave alone, he arranged for his sister Helen to take his two younger children for a while. Helen and Addie moved to Alvadore to live with their aunt and uncle. To get the older ones to school in Junction City, he enlisted his mother's help. James rented a house in town and Mother Bushnell gladly agreed to move there and stay with her two eldest grandchildren.

Once back out on the farm and all alone, James sat down by his desolate fireplace with the snow, ice and the gloom outside and began to realize what he had lost. At first there was so much ice outside that no one was able to move around. The only sound James heard outside was the sharp crack of breaking branches off the ice laden trees. The only living things he saw from morning until night were his cows and horses as he fed and took care of them. "O the long and dreary winter, O the sad and lonely days," he wrote in the journal he'd kept through most of his adult years. He'd started writing it during his times of loneliness on the Oregon Trail, away from his family that first year. He continued writing in it off and on when, like now, he was alone.

All things finally have an end and after seven weeks of constant snow on the ground, all the snow disappeared at long last. Then the daily routine of plowing, sowing, and harvesting arrived to fill up his time. The work helped fix his mind on other things. James built an addition to his house that summer and he proudly realized that this farmhouse would likely stand many decades. He next rented a part of his farm to Howard Haughman, a young man from Pleasant Hill who'd been working for James some of that long and dreary winter.

# CHAPTER EIGHTEEN

## *Elvan McClure Pitney*

### JULY 2, 1935

"GRANDMA, WHERE DID YOU get that?" asked eleven-year-old Elvan. He and his Grandmother Pitney were in her downstairs bedroom. She'd been living with his family at their farmhouse outside Junction City ever since he could remember. "It looks so old and ripped. Are you sure we should put it up?" He was watching his grandmother tenderly unpack a tattered star-spangled banner from her wood and metal-trimmed old trunk.

"Well, honey, it's from my father, James Bushnell, and it is very old. Our family has flown this flag ever since the Civil War and probably even before that."

"Wow," Elvan exclaimed. "The Civil War seems so long ago."

His grandmother chuckled and replied, "I'll always remember the day my father hung it outside our porch. It was the same year the war broke out back east. He called it our Liberty Pole. Father fiercely claimed that, as long as he was alive, we Bushnells would always stand for freedom—freedom for every person, regardless of religion or race. He strongly and often made that point to Charles and me. As a result, we children always clearly remembered on which side of the Civil War the Bushnells stood."

Lucy went on reminiscing about her father, young Elvan's grandfather. "He took out his Bible that same evening and read to us from the end of Galatians, chapter three, about all people being the same in Christ, with no racial or social differences. Then, he assured us that any church our family attended would always teach and believe those words from the Apostle Paul.

"We children needed to hear that, too, Elvan, because on the very next Sunday, Charles, Helen, and I heard some loud arguing going on among the men at church. We had started to exit, and I was shocked to hear one of our friends shouting that he would never be a part of our church again! It sounded to me like he was mad because most of the church folks didn't support his Confederate beliefs. This friend and all his family were from the South.

"I'd never heard grown men shout like that at each other. It got worse when that man picked up a chair and threw it at my father. Now, that really scared Helen and me and we got behind Charles but kept watching for what our dad would do. I remember grabbing Charles' arm just as Mama appeared to shoo us all out the front door. Mama was wide-eyed and acting plenty nervous as she got us in our wagon."

Elvan stared at his grandma in astonishment. "Did they really fight each other? Did your papa get in a big fight?" he asked.

"No, no, child. I did think that man or his son might have wanted to hit someone, but my father stayed very calm. Before we left the church, I heard Papa say to the group of men still there that he would never stop loving this man —-or any of his family. That they were brothers in Christ. However, Papa made it clear that they and any others of the Confederate opinion would have to keep quiet in church. He emphasized that our church would never condone slavery.

"On the way home Papa talked to us about the fight. He said this was a time when many people all over the United States had extraordinarily strong beliefs. Many strongly believed in freedom for all men and women; while others believed just as strongly in the rights of the landowners who needed slaves. I remember he explained that the war was being fought over those two beliefs. Since Papa would never agree with any notion of slavery, we Bushnells aligned with the North, or the Union as it was called.

"Then Mama spoke up and reminded us that Christian love is greater than any of men's disagreements. I knew Mama had been raised on her family's plantation with slaves in Virginia, so her saying that really impressed me. Papa agreed and he talked to us older kids about unity and a love that overlooks another's faults. Once we got home, he read that to us in the Bible, where Jesus taught His followers to not hate others or fight, and to not divide the church.

"Later, in school, Charles and I were shocked to learn that even out here in Oregon, some men were doing hateful things. They formed these Knights of the Golden Circle groups that went around on horseback at night in white robes and masks scaring and threatening anyone of a different race or sometimes a different religion. Sometimes they also threatened people who helped the ones they hated. When Charles or I asked Papa about the

Knights, he wouldn't tell us any of their names. He warned us that we'd hear different sides of the issue all over our own little community, each side believing they were right. But we were to always remember what the Bible said in Galatians 3:26-28 'You are all sons of Christ.' And 'There is neither Jew nor Greek, there is neither slave nor free, there is neither male nor female; for you are one in Christ Jesus.' I will always remember Papa getting out his old, black Bible and reading that to Charles and me.

"It was a sad, disturbing time during those years. So many grownups were getting angry at so many things. Then it became even more sad for our family. My baby brother, who we called Willie Francis, died right before he turned five years old."

"Oh, Grandma," Elvan moaned. "That's so very sad to lose a brother." He paused, quietly thinking about it.

"Well, dear, I had already lost two baby sisters before Willie died. And, yes, each time it was always very sad. One little sister only lived two weeks, so I never really got to know her. That was baby Mary Elisabeth, named after Mama. The very night that we buried baby Mary, our sweet little Josephine got very sick— and died just one month later. That was even harder for me, because she was so cute and happy, and I enjoyed her so much. She was just easy to love, and I liked taking care of her. Also, she was Papa's special little girl for those two years she was with us. When she died, I really thought it was the hardest on Papa. I remember he became very quiet for many months.

Both Elvan and Grandma sat silently, until she said, "Well, that's enough of that. We need to get this flag up and flying proudly from our porch." She stood, a tiny figure carrying the flag reverently in both hands outside her bedroom door. Elvan, already taller than his grandmother, was still thinking of those little ones dying as he followed her.

Two days later, Elvan brought it up again. The family had finished celebrating at Junction City's Fourth of July picnic and were resting at home. Elvan was sitting next to Grandmother Pitney near the fireplace with his hands holding her hank of yarn as she wrapped it into a ball. He decided to ask her what was on his mind.

"Grandma, did you have any other brothers or sisters die?"

"Well, yes I did," she said, seemingly surprised at his question. "I lost two more brothers. But before them, my own dear mother died. In fact, I was just a few years older than you, Elvan, about 14." She paused, but kept her hands busy, rolling the yellow yarn.

Elvan was surprised again. "Your mother died, too?" he stammered. "That's terrible."

"Yes, dear, it was awfully hard. And she was sick a long time before she died." Wide-eyed, Elvan watched as his grandmother went back in time as she spoke.

"We didn't have good medicines or doctors back then. So, people and children often didn't survive even the simple, common diseases. Life was more fragile, and many didn't live as long as we do now. Almost every family lost loved ones in those times. You can be very thankful that scientists and doctors have learned so much more since then.

"So, my mama, she got sick working out in the farm fields, helping put in our Spring crops. She chose to go outside and work. She liked to do that. So, when she went outside to work that time, she put me in charge of the house. I felt so grown up because she let me watch baby Addison and do the housework. She and Pa both treated me like I was an adult that spring. It was hard caring for the baby and overseeing my little sister Helen, but I tried not to complain—because I wanted them to keep treating me like a grownup. I even managed to get most of the housework done when the little ones slept." She paused. "Hmmm. I was so determined."

"Grandma, that sounds like a lot of work for you, but it is nice being treated like an adult," Elvan stated, but then nodded his head. "I know how I felt grown-up when Dad taught me how to drive our tractor and help with his work."

"Well, there you go. I really was doing fine at first, too" she recalled, "but then it got worse. After about two weeks, I first noticed that Mama started walking in more slowly from the fields. Then, I remember Papa insisted one evening that she come in earlier the next day. At first, she argued with him, but she seemed to get more tired each day. Soon, she started coming in earlier in the afternoon and then just sat holding the baby and resting by the fire. Sometimes she'd help me with supper. I remember how strange it felt, having more responsibility for supper than my own mother.

"One day after she came in, she couldn't seem to warm up. She was shivering and went to bed as soon as she ate. I was quite surprised she didn't resist the next morning when Papa told her to wait until later to come out, after the air had warmed up a bit. She went out late and came in early. I was glad to have her company for sure, but I couldn't help but worry at the changes I saw in her. She was tired so much of the time. Then, she caught a bad cold followed by a nasty cough a few days after that.

"Even though I was young, I essentially became Mama's nurse after she took to her bed day and night. Plus, I was still taking care of the two little ones. Again, I tried not to ever complain, but Papa saw that it was too much for me and sent for Grandmother Bushnell, who lived with Aunt Helen back then. Mama was unhappy that Papa did that and I was surprised when

Mama kept asking for my help instead of Grandmother. So, Grandmother took over the other chores while I cared for my Mama. It's a good thing we had Grandmother's help because Mama stayed in bed all the rest of that summer."

She stopped there.

"Then when did she die?" the boy prodded.

"Many months later."

Suddenly his grandmother clammed up. She reached for the yarn still left on his outreached hands and put it with her large ball in the knitting basket beside her. Then, she stood up, kissed him on the top of his head and said, "Good night, dear. I'm worn out."

# CHAPTER NINETEEN

## *James Meets Sarah*

**1869**

IN THE FALL, JAMES found a house to rent in Eugene and got his two oldest children started in high school there. He wanted those two to get a more thorough education than what Junction City offered. Also, James felt the farm was too remote. He couldn't easily get his children to school and back again, let alone from any type of activity after school. So, his mother agreed to supervise Charles and Nettie in Eugene and run the household there while his sister Helen minded the younger two children in Alvadore once again. James dutifully returned to his farm and spent another lonesome winter there. At least he didn't have the same severely cold weather to cope with again. That winter was much milder. Another sad occurrence happened in the spring, when he learned that his little two-year-old Addie hurt his spine while staying with Helen. His sister was quite distraught, and the family all felt terrible for the toddler and his aunt.

On January 1, 1870, his dear friends, Vincent and Sally McClure, helped James become acquainted with Mrs. Sarah Page. She was younger than him by almost 20 years, but she didn't seem at all concerned about their age difference. She was small with long, wavy brown hair and full of many smiles. Her smiles and laughter warmed his heart. His new relationship with Sarah blossomed into friendship and then grew into a strong commitment. On April 2, Sarah became his wife and as he proclaimed later in his journal, "the partner of all his joys and sorrows." She, too, had already experienced a good deal of trouble in her young life of 24 years. To start with, she was just an infant when her mother died. Sarah's aunt, Mrs. Sarah

Davidson, took her in and raised her as her own child, along with her own five children. Because of the loving woman Sarah became, James always claimed that Mrs. Davidson raised her extremely well. Also, when James met her, Sarah had already buried two husbands.

She was also actively raising two young children, each from a different father. Glenn O. Powell, aged four, was born to Sarah and Glenn Powell. Two-year-old Sarah Olive was the child of Sarah and James Page. These two children joined the Bushnell children, Charles, Nettie, Helen, and Addie, and made a new family. Their house on the farm now became a full and lively household and now James greatly appreciated that Sarah was younger and energetic. With Charles 18 years old and Nettie 15 years old, Sarah concentrated mainly on raising the four youngest children. However, she tried to befriend the older two in a loving and respectful manner. They all tried their best to adjust to their new family.

# CHAPTER TWENTY

## *The Big Railroad Junction*

THE SAME YEAR JAMES and Sarah were married, there was great excitement and soaring hopes when the Oregon-California Railroad came to Junction City. Railroad entrepreneur, Ben Holladay, arrived in town and claimed that the merely one-day train ride from Portland made Junction City the perfect joining spot between the Oregon-California Railroad and the Oregon Central line. He boisterously promised the townsfolk that "their little town would become the second Chicago." Holladay apparently believed it to be the future refueling station for both lines. Based on his conviction, he purchased 90 acres from T.A. Milliorn for his development. The locals all watched in awe as the railroad crews first built storage buildings, then a bunkhouse and a mess hall for the construction and railroad workers. Water tanks and acres of wood piles soon stood on the east side of the tracks. Holladay used more railroad funds to purchase more land from C.W. Washburn. Homes were built in town for the railroad's permanent employees. Holladay put up a roundhouse and turntable next. Then, he brought in Chinese repairmen and set them up with housing in the little town. Their colorful Oriental culture was thought to be an interesting addition to many, but not all accepted the foreigners. Everyone seemed to enjoy the Chinese New Year celebration, though, when candy and nuts were handed out and fireworks lit the skies.

The first train thundered into Junction on its way to Eugene on October 9, 1871. Many passengers got off and changed trains there. In little Junction City, big engines huffed and puffed, and the train crews slept, ate, worked their shifts, and lived there. It became a booming town! However, the boom was short-lived. Within a few months, all the exciting plans fizzled.

When the more prosperous residents of the larger Eugene City promoted a different route for the trains, a tremendous disappointment swept over James, Sarah, and their whole community. Eugene City raised enough money to lure the railroad line to them. Their proposal moved the bridge crossing the Willamette River closer to the town of Harrisburg and completely bypassed Junction City. The new Eugene route was quickly approved by the railroad company. Despite Holladay's previous claims, Junction City was soon bypassed as "the Chicago of the West" in favor of Eugene's vision—and money.

Holladay had exhausted all his funds by then, so he was bought out by Henry Villard. Villard finished the construction of the Southern Pacific. It was exciting for James and Sarah when the first train ran through Junction City all the way from San Francisco on its way to Portland. It was December 19, 1887. However, soon after the Chinese and other railroad employees left their new little railroad town. James, a loyal townsman, and a Junction City Council member by then, ached for their beloved city.

James and Sarah's discouragement over the railroad was soon replaced by the joyful birth of their first child. On November 3, 1871, a son was born whom they named Henry Clay, after the U.S. Senator of the same name. Sarah and James were both strong admirers of Senator Clay. They'd read many accounts that Clay was also greatly respected by Abraham Lincoln for his wisdom. Senator Clay had guided the country through many peaceful compromises before and during the war.

# CHAPTER TWENTY-ONE

## *An Exciting New Endeavor*

A WAVE OF NEW economic excitement hit the farmers in the Junction City area in the 1870's and James was affected. He always brought the latest news from the City Council meetings home to discuss with Sarah. One night he excitedly told her that German hop plants were being introduced and planted in the Willamette Valley. The hop enthusiasts claimed that the local climate and environment were comparable to the best hop lands in Germany. Plus, the valley's soil and ample water supply would provide the new crop with excellent growing conditions. The visitors came with proof, too. In their very own Lane County, neighbor George Leasur had produced the first successful hop harvest. That was over a year ago now.

James was always looking for new and better ideas to make money and joined right in with the current hop fever. He listened and learned along with the neighboring farmers about growing the new crop. He heard them say the plant's yeast was valuable and harvested in the late summer. Hop buyers were coming to town to meet with the farmers and made promises to buy up all the hops that the locals could grow.

So, James set about putting in his own hop yard on a few acres. He plowed the rows and used youthful Charles to follow along behind, mounding up small hills where each cone, or flower seed, would be planted. They stuck big ten-foot poles into each mound to allow for the vines to climb upward as they grew. Then, James and Charles painstakingly put one seed in each hill. They watered and waited for the plants to emerge. While waiting, James even hand-carved his own hop hoe. He had the head crafted so it perfectly fit his hand.

Months later, while at the Fourth of July community picnic, he and Sarah were enjoying tasty food, music and visiting friends while their children played in the group games. His brother William was in town visiting and he was also spread out on their blanket with them. As they all watched the games, before long they got to talking about the new hop crop. William happened to say, "I heard most of the buyers from Salem are using the hops to make beer."

"No, not around here." James shook his head. "Our hops are going for bread yeast. We've been told there is a real demand all over the nation for more yeast."

William looked confused. "Are you sure? Bread yeast? I just visited with a fellow in Salem who was all excited about the hops' market for flavoring beer. He sure had convinced me that's why farmers are growing hops. It's all over the middle Valley and especially here in Lane County."

"Oh, yes! I'm sure ours are going towards the bread-making market," replied James.

However, Sarah, who'd overheard the brothers' conversation, brought it up again on the way home. "You know, James, you better be sure who and what you're selling our hops to. It would be a shame, and I think a sin, to be working for the beer makers. We never want to get involved with that, even if it's just a mistake. The buyers may have avoided telling the good people around here their whole plan. Please double check to be sure before you sell to them."

"Okay, dear. I will check on it again for your sake," he said in a placating tone. He patted her knee as he drove the wagon home. She gave him a thin-lipped smile and a nod.

The next evening James came home from working in the town granary. Sarah had baked some fresh rolls and they made the whole house smell delicious. He sat down to supper, thanked the Lord for their meal and added a request to God for some special wisdom. They ate a noisy family meal that included a lot of the previous day's picnic leftovers.

Nettie and Helen were put in charge of the cleanup and James asked Sarah to sit a spell with him on the porch. With the little ones playing around their feet, James managed to tell Sarah his unfortunate news. "The word in town is that our hops are actually destined for the beermakers. Harry Johnson just learned the fact from his brother living in Salem. Yes, the buyers that came to Junction City are selling it only to brewers."

Sarah gasped. "Oh, no! That's terrible."

"I just can't believe that I was fooled so easily, Sarah. And I am so disappointed. I was looking forward to this new endeavor and now, all my joy feels like a big bubble that just burst in my face! Sarah, what am I going to do?" he moaned.

"Well, the best thing we can do now is pray for guidance, James." And they prayed together right then and there.

The next day they both agreed on what must be done. They were going to make a statement that the whole community would see. Believing that beer drinking caused too much damage to families, they would not assist in any way with the production of beer or any type of alcohol. With Charles helping him the next day, James began the demanding work of pulling out their young hop plants one by one. The plants were a good four to five feet tall now and it took strong muscle-power to get them out. Using the hop hoe with the specially carved handle, James and Charles took turns digging up and chopping the crop. By the end of the week, the Bushnell hop yard was a mess of dying plants and piles of dirt. Even though he was asked a few times, James refused to spare the plants by giving any of them away.

James became the talk of the town for many months after that and many folks laughed at his folly. For most, it was hard to fathom what he had done by digging up his whole crop, and they cast many critical judgments. Even though he was thoroughly embarrassed, he just carried on with his work and other responsibilities. From a few others — church friends mostly—there was some affirmation. As a church Elder, James had led by example in this very costly decision. Therefore, he and Sarah were both discouraged when no one else followed his lead.

# CHAPTER TWENTY-TWO

*Elvan M. Pitney, 11 years old*

## NOVEMBER 1, 1935

TODAY WAS HIS GRANDMOTHER'S 81st birthday and there would be some family coming to their farm to help celebrate. Elvan was excited because he'd see a few of his cousins. But first there were some extra chores to do. He was assigned to help his grandmother get the dining room table set. He knew the plates were heavy for her and he could help. He played marbles on the living room floor until his grandmother was ready. Once she came into the dining room, he swept his marbles up and dropped them into his leather pouch. Sticking it in his back pocket, he stood and walked over to the round dining table.

Grandma said, "Oh, I see you've already added the extra leaves to our table. That was smart of you, lad. Next, we'll put on the white lace tablecloth. That's my very favorite one and I think I can be choosy today, don't you?"

"Sure, Grandma," he smiled and replied. "That sounds quite right to me."

"Now, will you help me in my room, by lifting the trunk lid and holding it open as I dig out the cloth?" He started towards her bedroom in response and got the lid up before his tiny grandmother even got into the room. She always walked very slowly. He held up the top of the wooden trunk as she uncovered a few things and pulled out the lacey tablecloth, and then he shut it carefully again.

She never locked it, but he thought it had an interesting metal lock. So, he asked "Do you have a key for this trunk somewhere, Grandma? Do you ever lock it?"

She looked at him through her tiny glasses and nodded. "Yes, there's a key I keep in with my jewelry over there," and she gestured to their left. "However, the only times I've ever locked it were when I was traveling somewhere. I locked it when I moved to Monmouth for college. And then one other time when I went by train to stay with Aunt Jemima a few weeks in Eugene. I helped her with their children when she was quite ill. Other than that, I've had no need to really keep it secure." She slowly turned back to the long hallway heading towards their dining room, and Elvan followed.

Once back in the dining room, they spread the lace cloth over the table and began using their hands to smooth out the wrinkles. Elvan asked, "I've been thinking about your mother dying when you were just 14. I didn't realize you had two mothers."

There was silence as Grandmother straightened up and stretched her back. She responded without smiling, "I didn't really have two mothers. At least it didn't feel that way to me. I was 16 when our friends, the McClures, introduced my Papa to Sarah Page. You should always remember those dear friends, Elvan, since that is your middle name— "McClure." The McClure family became very special to my mother when they crossed the Oregon Trail together. Once they all made it to the Willamette Valley, Mama and Papa settled on a land claim close to the McClures, also."

"Anyway, after they introduced Sarah to my father and I met her, I thought she seemed quite young compared to him. And she was only seven years older than I was! But she had already been widowed twice. They met right after Christmas. Sarah had two children and Papa thought she was quite wonderful from the very start. They courted while I was at school living with my grandmother in Eugene. Your Uncle Charles, whom you never knew, also lived with us in Eugene. Grandmother told us that Papa was courting and thinking about getting married again. Charles and I were both quite surprised at the thought of it," she chuckled. "We thought Papa was too old to get married. However, in April they had a wedding in the Junction City Christian Church. That's the church your grandpa started and helped grow. It's a good-sized church now but it wasn't much back then.

"When they got married, Sarah's little boy Glenn, your Uncle Glenn, was only 4 years old. His sister Ollie, your Aunt Olive, was just 2. Sarah had her hands full with her two little ones, plus our little Addie and Helen, who were 5 and 8 at the time. They still needed a mother, but Charles and I were sure we were fine and too old to need another mother. He was 18 and I was 15. Charles and I finished up the school year in Eugene that Spring and then moved back home once school was out. It wasn't easy leaving our school friends that first winter, but Papa didn't give us any choice in the matter. Back to Junction City we went.

"When we moved back to the old house for the summer, I was needed quite a bit to help Sarah with the younger children. After two years living apart from the younger ones and our Papa, Charles and I were both glad to be back together as one family. However, it was never the same. It felt so strange and at first it was hard for me to get used to all the changes. Sarah was nice enough to me when she wasn't too busy with the little ones, and she accepted that Charles and I didn't really need her to be a mother to us. She was truly kind and helpful to me but was more like an older friend than a mother. That was the trick for us: staying friends in such a chaotic and noisy household of little ones.

"Looking back to that summer, Elvan, it was quite an adjustment. I had gotten used to living and going to school in Eugene. You know that's a much bigger city, right?"

"Yes. I really like it when we go to Eugene!" he jumped in. "There are so many more stores and streets there. I can't even imagine how fun it would be to live around kids my own age. I don't have even one friend in the same grade around here."

"Well, you're right, Elvan. Eugene was fun," she agreed. "But it was also fun to be with both my brothers and my sister Helen again, too. I'd missed Helen quite a bit.

"We children were finally back together all under one roof, but it was a crowded home and way out in the country. You see, I had gotten used to seeing my friends in the city every day. So, I started riding my horse once a week to my friends' house from out on the farm. Also, I'd meet up with some of my friends at church on Sundays. That was about it for my social life that summer, so I eagerly looked forward to school starting in the Fall. Then, when it did, I was surprised that Junction City high school was so much smaller to me now. It seemed to have shrunk in size. But I had many of my same old friends there, at least, and that really helped me.

"When Charles went on to college in Monmouth that Fall, and I missed him every day. It was the right time for him to go to college, but I just wasn't ready for him to leave. He'd always been such a good brother to me. We had grown up together, just the two of us, for many, many years, and now he wasn't around like he'd been all my life. But then, even worse, he unexpectedly died two years after he went off to college," she sighed.

Elvan couldn't stay quiet at this news. "What!? You lost another brother?" When Grandmother didn't answer right away, he asked more softly, "How did he die?"

"He caught a disease, something in his lungs they called consumption. Now they would call it tuberculosis and we have a way of curing it. Not back then, though. It was the same illness my mother caught and battled until she eventually died. Charles struggled with that disease for two years before he came back home to Junction City to die." She paused in her own thoughts and stood still at the table. "He had been my best friend my whole life long, Elvan. I was as sad about losing him as I had been about losing my mother. We had helped each other get through the loneliness after Mother's death. And when Father sent us to live with Grandmother, we only had each other. Charles was an incredibly good big brother."

Elvan didn't know what to say. He was sad for his grandmother.

Nettie stirred herself into action and started neatly folding the napkins in half. "Well, life certainly didn't stand still for me. In a few months after school started again, Sarah and Papa had a new little baby boy. They named him Henry Clay. I think that name was after a famous southern senator that they both admired. He was a cute, happy baby and delighted us all. It was a lot more work for Sarah, though, and I usually came right home from school and took over caring for the youngest children— Addie, Glenn, and Ollie. They were all under six years old and too noisy for Sarah and the new baby sometimes. I know for sure they were too noisy for me!

"I lived with Papa and Sarah until I went off to Oregon Christian College in Monmouth the next year. So, you see, I didn't really have another mother. I lived with Sarah for less than two years. I well remember and love my Mama- Elisabeth was her name- dearly. I don't think Papa ever forgot my mother, but I know he loved Sarah very much, too. To me, they seemed happy together and, despite their age difference, well-matched.

"Oh, dear! These plates are so heavy. Please spread them around the table, Elvan, and then I'll follow with the silverware. I've spent too much time talking."

"But, Grandma, I really like your stories. And I learned a lot about our family. I sure hope I never have to have another mother," he added vigorously.

"So do I, grandson. Always be thankful for the one you have," and with that she stopped talking.

# CHAPTER TWENTY-THREE

## *James and Sarah*

**1874**

THE SUMMER PASSED BY pleasantly and prosperously, with no premonition of the sad, sad winter which was to follow. After packing her wooden trunk with its shiny metal trim, Lucy Jennette went away to school in Monmouth that September. Because she was his eldest daughter, James had given Nettie her mother's wooden trunk, and it was very special to the 18-year-old.

In November another baby was born to Sarah and James, but sadly, was quickly returned to "the Giver of all good gifts," as James said.

By 1874, James' eldest, Charles Alvah, had suffered much with the dreaded consumption for two or three years. After being in school at Monmouth's Christian College for two years, Charles tried going to live in the mountains to improve his health. He stayed one winter on the McKenzie River, but it was of no-good result. He still went downhill gradually. He was just 23 years old with such a bright and promising life ahead of him. It was extremely hard for James to watch his son have to give up on life just when Charles was coming into manhood. James knew that if it were not for the hope given them in the Gospel, he'd be unable to comfort Charles. However, for Charles, it seemed the grave held no terror. The young man had long before made "the Friend of Sinners" his friend, so he was not afraid. With his summons from God calling him away soon, Charles asked his father to read the Bible to him. He specifically wanted to hear what Christ said about many mansions and going to prepare a place for him. Charles seemed truly comforted by these promises as James read them. When his dear sister, Nettie, came home from college, Charles gave her and James his few earthly possessions, bid his family goodbye, and calmly and fearlessly passed from Earth's waters to the Heavenly shore. It was an exceedingly difficult load for James to bear when he had to lay his son's lifeless body down in the cold and silent grave.

It helped comfort James, Sarah, and the whole family when G. M. Whitney preached to the large, sorrowful, and sympathetic circle of the Bushnell family and friends at Charles' funeral. Brother Whitney used Job's old question, "'If a man die, shall he live again?' Triumphantly, the question was answered when Jesus Christ arose from the dead and brought life, light, and immortality through the Gospel. From henceforth when our dear ones are laid away in the silent tomb we do not sorrow as those who have no hope for if Jesus died and rose again, we know that those who are asleep in Him will God bring with Him and we shall be caught up with Him The Lord and enjoy His presence and those of our loved ones forever."

## A LITTLE TOWN GROWS

Soon after the railroad excitement, Junction City was incorporated on October 29, 1872. There was a population of 600 people. The first ordinance passed by the City Council authorized the building of a wooden sidewalk from the "drug store to the meat market" on Front Street. However, those were the only sidewalks completed for many years.

In the spring of 1874, James and three other men built a grain warehouse in the young town, on Front Street right close to the railroad storage tanks. Even though the town never became a rail hub, the railroad's convenience caused Junction City to become the receiving town for crops from the vast farming area. Soon there were a total of five big warehouses standing in town.

James' partners were O.R. Bean, William Edward, and Pat Breeding. The partners chose James as the one to go up north to Portland that spring and make the arrangements for shipping their grain up to Portland. Also, he was supposed to buy all the burlap sacks they needed. Given the opportunity, James quickly decided that Sarah must go to the city with him. Charles' death was still lingering sadly over their family and James wanted to give Sarah a break from her daily routines. Nettie had gone back to school a week after Charles' funeral. Without Nettie's help, Sarah had her hands full again with their five children still at home. On top of all that, Sarah moved through her days now with a heavy and sorrowful heart. With all this in mind, James arranged for his mother to come and stay in their home for the two days and one night they'd be gone. Sarah insisted that she couldn't be gone any longer than that.

After giving lots of instructions to Mother Bushnell and some to their daughter, Helen, who now preferred to be called Jennie, they all headed to the station one crisp morning. On the departure platform, the parents quickly gave many goodbye hugs and kisses. Then, James eagerly assisted Sarah up the two steep steps and they were both aboard the Portland-bound train. Settling into their appointed smooth, red upholstered seats, they found they had a compartment all to themselves. Sarah automatically chose the best window seat and frantically started waving to their children jumping all around James' mother. The cold lunch packed in a bag was hastily set beside their one suitcase laying on the bench seat across from them. Still waving goodbye, the Bushnells heard the long, piercing whistle and the train started up with a sudden lurch. Off plopped both bags down onto the floor! They both laughed out of embarrassment and James set the luggage upright again, but this time on the floor.

It wasn't long after they left Junction City and had passed through neighboring Harrisburg, that Sarah said, "I'd like to go explore the rest of this car. Will you watch our bags? I'll be gone for just a bit." James agreed with a smile and a nod as he continued reading *The Oregonian* newspaper given to them by the conductor. It wasn't more than five minutes when Sarah returned. She had nothing much to report; just a few other passengers and none that she knew. She settled into the knitting project she'd brought along, although she did much more looking out her window than knitting. She marveled aloud, "The valley fields are such beautiful shades of green. So many different shades of greens are quite a sight. I love the colors of the trees, too. Just brilliant. It's scenes like this that make me wish I were a painter. Though nobody is ever quite the artist that our God is, but I'd still like to try it someday."

James just listened. After about an hour, he took a turn to stretch his legs. He easily struck up a conversation with another man who lived in Halsey, and they compared the commerce and farming situations in their towns. By the time he came back to sit down, James was feeling proud of the advancements of Junction City as compared to those of Halsey. The new eastern railroad had also bypassed this little town as it crossed the new bridge on its way to Eugene. At least, Junction City still had a thriving train depot and business center.

Their train stopped in Salem for about 30 minutes, and they enjoyed perusing the lovely station. Back on board and after their noon meal, this pattern of each separately taking a stretch was repeated. Neither gathered much more news, though. The only other stop was briefly in Oregon City, which was still a bustling town after all the years since James was last there. That had been about 20 years ago on his second time traveling down the Willamette Valley while searching for his family. Coming from the south this time, he was able to get a magnificent view of Willamette Falls and really appreciate their power and beauty.

From Oregon City, it was nonstop on into Portland. Here, the big city's two-story wooden and brick train station was quite impressive to the small-town couple. The long passenger platform was the largest either James or Sarah had ever seen. It was also the busiest they'd ever seen! Keeping a tight grip on each other and their bags, they disembarked slowly. They stopped a moment while James stood on the platform and sought out which direction they needed to head. Neither he nor Sarah were tall people, so he knew better than to merge into the crowd without knowing the right direction. He spied the carriages for hire and led Sarah towards them. Leaving his business tasks for tomorrow, James wanted this to be their night to enjoy some new sights together. He chose a carriage and instructed their driver to the boarding house in the Skidmore district that Brother Whitney had recommended.

After checking into that very friendly and lovely establishment, they left their bags and confirmed their dinner time. Then, they started off for a walk. It was mild and pleasant for an April afternoon and there were fragrant flowering trees planted along the streets. They strolled along the riverside and into one of the landscaped parks they came upon. They stopped to sit on a wrought iron bench and enjoy the scenic riverside park for a few minutes. James heard Sarah peacefully sigh. He smiled to himself, realizing that she was finally able to relax and enjoy it here. He was so glad.

Returning to their lodging, they discovered the dining room food and the company of fellow travelers to be quite nice. Thankful to Brother Whitney, they appreciated that their fellow travelers were both genteel and pleasant. Sarah had worried some over this situation before setting out from home and now she was much relieved, and so was James.

Besides the strange bed and stranger city noises, they enjoyed their one-night stay in Portland. Sarah didn't want to stay behind alone the next morning when James headed out to the shipping warehouses. So, they leisurely enjoyed a fine breakfast together in the dining room and then packed up their belongings. The hostess called out for a driver and their bags were carried for them out to an awaiting carriage. Off they headed to the shipping depository along the muddy Willamette River. The river was much deeper and wider here in Portland than in Eugene and Sarah enjoyed just watching it flow. James said the muddiness reminded him of the Mississippi back in Hannibal.

In the warehouse district, they found the business they were looking for. The granary owner greeted them amiably and was delighted to show them around his huge warehouse and loading docks. When they entered the immense area where the sacks were being stitched and finished, James was surprised to learn he had several choices. He had to choose from four different types of burlap. He cautiously chose the middle grade with the middle price tag attached. After placing his order, using their business account and address of the same, the sacks were guaranteed to be shipped within the next business week. James and Sarah left feeling secure that their burlap sacks would reach Junction City as promised.

Now, it was time to catch the late morning train; the last to leave with a guarantee to reach home before 6:00 p.m. They climbed abroad and settled into a compartment like their first one. This time they shared it with a single gentleman also heading south. He was a Eugene resident, and it didn't take long for them to learn he knew James' brother, John Corydon! As much younger men, their new friend had worked on the Skinner's Ferry along with Cory. Cory's first job after settling in Lane County was on the ferry. This man knew both Cory and his wife, Jemima, from their McKenzie Forks Baptist Church. After living in several other places, Cory's family was farming the Tandy farm now. Talking about his brother made James realize it'd been too long since he'd seen his brother's family.

**Railroad and Bushnell Warehouse**

# CHAPTER TWENTY-FOUR

THE BUSHNELL'S GRAIN WAREHOUSE was completed in time for the harvest and the farmers soon filled it to overflowing. As with much of their life, the promising season would soon take an unexpected turn.

Early that fall came a long rainy season which soaked the ground and made it extremely soft. Unbeknownst to James and his partners, their warehouse foundation was defective and the blocks upon which it stood soon swayed to one side. Eventually, within the week, the warehouse collapsed with its load of about 30,000 bushels of wheat in burlap sacks. The falling walls and sacks crushed the rest of the foundation, leaving the foundation blocks bulging up through the floor. All this destruction ripped open their grain sacks— from the bottom stacks clear up to the top ones. The four owners went to work over several days and nights and finally got all their grain shipped to Portland in good shape. Due to the pleasant weather amidst this disaster, very little wheat was lost. James and Sarah praised God.

As if undaunted, James went about rebuilding his warehouse using as many of the old timbers as he could salvage. His partners helped when they could, but James carried the bulk of the workload. The costs were divided equally for the rebuilding, but James got credit for doing much of the labor.

Unfortunately, though, when their warehouse had fallen, it struck another warehouse to its south belonging to William Lemon. That one was knocked flat. Fortunately, Lemon had little wheat in it. Still, his warehouse had to be rebuilt and James helped him finance the unexpected costs of the reconstruction.

James and Sarah had talked many times about building a house in the city so they could be closer to their warehouse business. Now as they were faced with rebuilding the warehouse, it seemed to James, the dreamer, that it was a suitable time to add the building of a house, too. He spoke about his idea to Sarah.

"Right before the winter you want to build a new house?" she queried skeptically.

"Well, just a simple structure to get us moved into town while we work at getting the new warehouse completed. Simple at first. Then, I'll add some more rooms as quickly as possible after that," James calmly explained.

"Hmm? And just how simple of a structure are you thinking about?"

"I'm thinking of two rooms for now," he slowly replied.

"What?" Sarah's voice rose. "For a family of seven? Nettie is off to college, but that's only one gone from our family. You can't possibly be thinking of all of us in the same bedroom? Can you?" She dragged those last words out slowly. Her arms had moved to each hip, and she stared at him as if he had gone crazy. "Well, whatever you're thinking, there's no possible way that I will move into just a two-room house," she declared.

Thinking quickly, James improvised with, "What if I put in a big sleeping loft for all the children? And add a new cook stove for you in the eating area?"

Sarah just sighed.

They bought a half block in the southwest corner of town and the building commenced. Often making James repeat his promise of adding more rooms once the warehouse was completed, Sarah began preparations to move into town. As soon as the two rooms and a loft were finished, the family of seven squeezed into the crowded new quarters right before Christmas.

It started raining as soon as they began moving in and it kept raining all that winter.

# CHAPTER TWENTY-FIVE

## 1875

BY THE NEXT SUMMER, after only one year, his partners grew dissatisfied with the grain business and sold out to James. When the transactions were completed, James was the sole owner of the local grain warehousing business. He hired Mr. Terpenning and his wife to live on his farm and work it while James and his family stayed in town. The Terpennings had proven to be good workers last year and he trusted them like family.

Adjacent to James' warehouse, William Lemon had rebuilt his demolished warehouse and added a large grain elevator to it. Within two years, Lemon was owing quite a sum on his building repairs and his new elevator; more than what James had covered for him. When Mr. Lemon finally confided to James that he had nothing to pay towards these debts, the two men devised a plan. James agreed to take Lemon's warehouse and steam engine for $6,500. That money allowed Lemon to pay off most of his debts.

After these transactions, James told Sarah "I feel as though we're being steered into the grain business and doing it all: storing, buying and shipping." And just as he predicted, in the Spring of 1876 every step of the grain business was now owned by the Bushnells.

Junction City was building up very quickly. There was now a large flour mill owned by Mr. Kratz, Mr. Howard, and Charles W. Washburne; two fine hotels; five large warehouses; a harness shop; several stores; and other miscellaneous shops. In the fall of 1876, James was elected to the City Council and served for the next four years, becoming the city's mayor the latter two.

One day James went to collect his weekly $2,000 at the Wells Fargo Express office. It was payday for his men at the warehouse. He walked the few steps from his warehouse to the depot and the Express office and then back again. At the end of the day when it was time to pay his workers, James frantically couldn't find the money. He searched all over his office. Then, he retraced his steps back from the Wells Fargo office. With still nothing found on his route, he finally ordered all the machinery shut down and told everyone what had happened. All his employees were told to begin searching all over the place. Shouts went up when one man looked in an empty nail keg and found the lost bag of money! James was relieved and happy. However, as he told Sarah at home, he couldn't understand how it had gotten there. He didn't want to suspect any dishonest employee, so they prayed about it and gave the situation to God. Then, James was able to relax and let the issue go.

Sarah and James welcomed a new baby boy on January 24, 1877. They named him Albert. However, despite their prayers and loving care, this dear one never really thrived or grew strong. In October, his pure spirit took its flight back to God and the family grieved the loss of their little nine-month-old.

Just a year later, on November 9, 1878, a bright and beautiful little girl was given to them. They named her Mary Josephine and rejoiced as this baby appeared to be very healthy.

# CHAPTER TWENTY-SIX

## *Mysterious Fires*

ON A FINE, CLEAR October day in 1878, Sarah was in her kitchen cleaning up from lunch. She was dreaming about sneaking in her own nap while her little boy was napping. She'd had a hard night and an early morning. Plus, she was heavy into her eighth month of pregnancy and continually tired. Sweeping in her kitchen, she was startled to hear the town's fire bell begin loudly clanging — and keep on clanging. Not worrying about three-year-old Walter sleeping in the bedroom, she quickly walked out to their porch, still holding her broom. She searched the sky for signs of smoke, first looking over and around the schoolhouse, because that's where three of her children were. She was relieved to see the sky in that direction was clear. Walking to the other end of her porch, she saw smoke coming from over by Front Street. And, just then, she saw two neighbor men running in that direction. She saw that first group meet other men who were yelling out alarms as they drove horses and wagons away from that area. Her closest neighbor, Mr. Roberts, burst out from his back porch with one bucket in hand and went into his shed, bringing out another. Sarah called out, "You can grab our buckets, too, Ray!" and he nodded to her but kept right on running.

Within five minutes though, Ray was back for the two buckets that Sarah had already brought out onto her porch. He panted, "Salomon's Store has caught on fire and there's big danger of the fire spreading!" He turned quickly and that's all she learned. That is, until school was let out and kids started yelling and running down the street. She heard her children before she saw them. They rounded the corner and came clamoring noisily up the steps. Once on the porch, Sarah quieted them down a bit and gave instructions. "Jennie and Glenn, go over two blocks and see what you can from the corner. Then, come back and tell us."

So, off the two oldest ran. That set Addie to complaining: "I'm just as old as Glenn and I shouldn't have to stay home!" Thus, with her consent, he started limping after his siblings who were long gone ahead of him. Sarah watched him move painfully and slowly down the steps and across the yard. She worried as she watched him go, because of his constant neck and back pain. It seemed that his old childhood injury was bothering him more lately.

Within minutes, the three older Bushnells ran home together breathlessly reporting that the fire had already burned the Mercantile and was starting to destroy the hotel now, too. Jennie told Sarah she'd seen James working hard amongst the other fire fighters. "He ordered us to get home and get out of the way." she glumly said.

Sarah responded, "Well, I'm sure that was just for your own safety."

James had sent his dirty coat home with them and Sarah immediately tasked Jennie to hang it on the side porch to air it out. It smelled terribly smoky! With younger children, including a toddler, to keep distracted inside, Sarah really didn't mind when she saw the older three sneak back to the corner lot and stand watch over there again. However, seven-year-old Henry was quick to tattle that his big brothers and sister had gone back outside to watch. It was obvious that the tattling was because he desperately wanted to go join them. She gave in and sent Henry and his big sister, Ollie, outside with strict orders "to remain only at the corner and go no farther— no matter what!"

Jennie ran back within a few minutes to report that now the Arlington Hotel and its ice cream parlor were completely gone. She also said James had called for Glenn to come help the firefighters and the boy had run off to do so. The mother and daughter looked at each other, but both remained silent. They had two family members fighting the fire, now. Finally, Sarah just sighed and kept cutting up her apples. She sent Jennie back with a chair for Addie and a cool cloth that might help the struggling lad's sore neck.

The fire had not completed its destruction with the burning of the ice cream parlor, however. Following the hotel, most of the town's business section was ablaze, also, and many houses were consumed. Four of the five city grain elevators and warehouses also burned, even with the townsmen fighting their hardest to douse the flames. James and Glenn fought hard, too, but unfortunately were up-close witnesses to the destruction of many of their town's buildings. The other four children watched from the corner and were stunned to see their own family's warehouse and grain elevator collapse and burn all the way to the ground. Then, horrified, they heard and watched the oil tanks of the Southern Pacific Railroad go up in black, smoky explosions. The Bushnell warehouse had been constructed awfully close to the railroad. Now, with hindsight, James realized that it may have been a mistake and quite unfortunate for many people.

Everything happened so quickly. Scarcely had the fire burned down to smoldering embers and the oily blasts died away, when a few men began working to clean up the blackened downtown. Others were starting to return home when the fire bell rang again! Mr. Boland, the schoolteacher, had sounded the alarm because he'd noticed flames in a corner of the schoolhouse. James and Glenn had already started for home, but now took off running in the other direction with their buckets still in hand, followed closely by the other four children. However, when their father saw them take off, with Addie in the rear, he turned and hollered, "You kids need to stay at this corner and watch from here. No closer, you hear?" He waited for them to turn back and demanded a response. "And Jennie's in charge. You understand?" James got some murmurs in response that he ignored and looked his 16-year-old daughter in the eye. She said, "I understand, Father."

Immediately James raced off to catch up with Glenn and the other men headed towards their wooden schoolhouse. Other townsfolk were already there, swinging damp burlap bags in attempts to smother the flames along the western wall. Water buckets were being hastily filled from a pump in a neighbor's yard. A few men were going into other nearby backyards to fill more buckets. Thanks to Mr. Boland's early discovery, this blaze was quickly extinguished, and the schoolhouse still stood at the end of that terrible day. Glenn, Jennie, Addie, Ollie and Henry hovered together in shock and stared at their marred and blackened school. The walls were scorched, with wet ashes covering most of the floor. Many of the desks and most of the books were damaged by the smoke and water.

Mr. Borland soon declared that this fire was clearly caused by arson, as was the Front Street fire. Gasoline-soaked rags were detected in the smoking rubble. When the news spread that both recent fires looked to have been deliberately set, it dazed the townspeople. Who would do such a disastrous thing to harm their town?

Still in shock and dismay, many weary men and a few women returned downtown the next day, determined to start the cleanup. It took many days for the community to assess all the tragic destruction and contemplate the significance of the events. Most of the town's commercial center would have to be rebuilt. A daunting task. All this damage and the suspicious circumstances causing it left a huge cloud of gloom hanging over the town.

However, no one was killed or even seriously harmed in the fires. That caused much happy rejoicing and praising God in the town's two churches that Sunday. But the financial damage was great. The losses from all the burned buildings throughout the city totaled $55,375. Supplies were donated from local citizens and nearby communities to help begin the rebuilding process. Insurance companies also came through with finances to help the community recover.

Despite the tragic mood in town, the Bushnells had the joy of planning the first wedding for one of their children. Lucy Jennette had accepted the proposal of William Pitney, a young local widower who'd grown up on a farm south of town. He had taught school for several years, was the town's recorder, and most recently had gone to work in the Bushnell's granary. Nettie always thought that she would have enjoyed being a teacher, but when she graduated from teacher's college, there were no open positions around Junction City. She also felt she needed to stay close to her father and help in the house full of children. So, she had stayed home in Junction City after finishing at Monmouth College. When William's wife died, he was left to raise his baby son. Nettie had gotten reacquainted with William through Grange activities. Later, he encouraged her efforts in the town's first library, by helping her haul many donated books and working alongside her as she organized them. They had spent over a year getting to know each other better and Nettie was pleased that her father increasingly entrusted his own business responsibilities to William.

Just four months later, another fire broke out in the town. At 3:30 a.m. on the morning of February 6, 1879, the dreaded fire bell began to ring. Again! James staggered out of bed and did his best to not awaken their three-month-old baby sleeping in the cradle nearby. He quickly pulled on pants and boots, grabbed his coat off the hook by the backdoor and rushed out to the street. At the corner, he saw that J. H. Berry's large hotel was burning, on the northwest corner of Front Street. The fire quickly consumed the hotel and all its contents that early morning. Then it spread and took out two saloons owned by J. E. Williams and the Craigs, plus the saddle and harness shop run by J.H. Heath. Once again, the whole town was in shock and disbelief. Someone was deliberately starting these fires! Why would someone want to cause such horrific destruction?

After a year and a half of peace, a fourth fire destroyed Howard's warehouse on August 10, 1880. Fortunately, Mr. Howard only had 300 bushels of grain in storage at the time. Usually, his warehouse contained closer to 150,000 bushels valued at $17,000. This was some consolation for the Howard family.

Tragically, just a year and half later, on March 23, 1882, the Kratz, Washburne, and Howard mill and their grain warehouse, both situated south of town, were both burned with all their contents, including a large quantity of flour and several thousand bushels of wheat. This fine steam mill had cost them nearly $30,000 to build and was now just blackened timbers and ashes.

The mysterious arsonist struck again on April 3. This time Louis Salomon's grain warehouse was deliberately set on fire and burned to the ground, with considerable wheat inside. It stood within six feet of James' warehouse. Fortunately, the Bushnell warehouse was mostly empty, and that space provided room to fight the fire inside by dashing water on the inner walls and pouring water over the roof. This frantic work saved James' warehouse from complete destruction. James remained eternally grateful for the protective work done by his friends and fellow townsmen, who were also assisted by the wind, which changed direction and blew the fire away from the building. In the end, the warehouse only lost the north roof and one northside wall.

This was the town's sixth fire. The Bushnell's warehouse fire turned out to be the last one for a good many years. Although it was well-documented that all these fires were of suspicious origin, neither the arsonist nor the motive was ever discovered. No viable suspect was ever brought to the City Council's attention. The fallout was harsh. Insurance companies considered Junction City too great a risk and wouldn't endorse any policies for a good year.

# CHAPTER TWENTY-SEVEN

*Elvan McClure Pitney, age 12*

## 1936

IT WAS A BRIGHT, cool, and unusually pleasant January afternoon. The Pitney family headed back home in their old blue Buick with Jim and Elvan in the back seat on both sides of Grandmother Bushnell. She was so small that she fit nicely between them. The family had been to the Neilsons' wedding in Junction City. Elvan went to weddings mostly hoping for a good piece of cake and some punch after the ceremony. He wasn't much interested in the girls' dresses, flowers or the bride and groom's vows. Sometimes there was some music he enjoyed. And sometimes there were even little sandwiches or something extra special just for the guests. He'd never forget the wedding when all the guests were given their own bag of mints, in addition to a serving of cake and punch. That one had been a boy's dream come true!

This wedding was alright. There were two songs, and the preacher hadn't talked very long. Elvan made it through without resorting to playing Hangman. He had stuck a pencil and paper in his pocket back home, just in case. He and Jim had managed not to start laughing either, not like the last wedding they'd gone to. During that wedding there'd been a fly that kept bothering the groom. The nervous young man kept shooing it away from his face. While doing that shooing, the groom accidently knocked his bride's veil askew. The minister had to stop the ceremony until the bride could get her veil straightened up again. Elvan thought that had been hilarious and started chuckling, and then Jim started snickering, too, and the next thing they knew both boys had a bad set of giggles. He really had tried to settle down after getting a very stern look from his dad. But then, he'd made the mistake of looking over at Jim and they both started laughing all over again. Their folks did not think the boys were funny at all and they were sent to their room once they got home. However, at today's wedding, everything went smoothly for the bride and groom and thus for the Pitney boys.

As they bumped along Junction's streets, Grandmother said "This was a lovely day for a winter wedding. I remember my own January wedding and that was a lovely day, too. You always take a chance on the weather here in the Willamette Valley, no matter what month you get married.

Elvan hadn't ever thought about his grandmother being young enough to be a bride. He knew something about her childhood, because she told him a few stories about the crowded cabins she'd lived in with all her brothers and sisters. Still, her being in a wedding gown or getting married had never occurred to him. With his mind running along that surprising new thought, he had to know more. "So, who did you marry again, Grandmother?" he asked. He was surprised that Jim burst out laughing and his parents riding up front even chuckled. Now, he was kind of embarrassed, but not really sure why.

Grandmother smiled warmly at him and said, "I was married to your grandfather, William Pitney. But you never knew him, did you, Elvan?" and patted the younger boy's knee. She turned towards Jim for a bit and Elvan really hoped she gave his big brother a stern look that said, "Be nice!"

"When I came back to live in Junction City after college, I spent most days helping Sarah with the younger children. But then Papa suggested that I start a library at our church, because I've always loved books and reading and writing. So, I gathered up donated books from all over town. Sometimes I'd get so many that I had to borrow a wheelbarrow from Papa's granary to haul them over to the church. I was busy and life kept moving along. Still, my parents encouraged me to go to the Grange meetings so I could enjoy making more friends. Up until then, church had been the best time to see my friends, but I did begin thinking it would be nice to do something different. So, I started joining my parents going to their Grange meetings and I was nicely surprised to see there were a few younger adults like me attending, also. I found I really enjoyed all their interesting events, especially the dances, potlucks and occasional speakers. Always be willing to try something new, boys." Again, she turned to look at both Jim and Elvan.

"I soon became a regular member and was talked into helping with the voluntary secretary job. Well, I had some spare time and liked getting out of the house and away from tending to the youngsters, if truth be told. So, I started going to the Grange's monthly executive meetings, too, and taking notes for everyone. It was at one of those night meetings that William Pitney offered me a ride home. He was the vice president of the group and seemed kind and quite funny He often told jokes and made comments in our meetings that made me laugh. This was surprising to me since his wife, Josephine, had died just a year before. I'd expected he might still be sadly recovering from that terrible loss. I especially liked how he always talked so fondly of his baby son, Royal— or Rory— as he nicknamed him. I couldn't help but notice what an especially loving father he was. He was also a teacher at the Oak Grove School and a farmer.

I took him up on his offer of a ride home. We talked about his teaching at first. Then, he told me a few funny stories about trying to raise Rory without any help. Apparently, after one long month on his own, he finally agreed to let his mother and sister, Melvina, help him with the baby. Of course, with their help it was a lot easier for William to get back to teaching and tending to his farm. His mother stayed day and night most weeks for several months.

I think William started to get lonely out on the farm because he moved into town. I was really surprised when my father casually mentioned one night at dinner that he was hiring William to work in our grain elevator. William would start once the school let out. It wasn't long after William started work in the granary that Father realized that he was good with numbers and other business details. Within six months, Father started turning more of the warehouse responsibilities over to William. And now that he was working with my father, I started to see William more often in town and not just at the Grange meetings. And I did like that." She paused here and smiled to herself.

Elvan noticed that their blue Buick had slowed down to a stop. Clarence, his father, interrupted them and said, "Mom and I are going into the grocery store. Who wants to go in with us?" Jim jumped out of the car immediately. Elvan hesitated, to see what his grandmother was going to do. She looked at the younger boy and said, "I'd rather wait right here."

"Sounds good to me, too. I'll wait here," Elvan said to his parents' retreating backsides. He'd decided to keep his grandmother company and keep asking her questions. He liked the stories she told about her younger days and now, the ones about his grandfather, too.

The lad turned to his grandmother, "What happened when you started seeing Grandpa in town?"

"Well, let me see. . .." she responded slowly. "I think it wasn't long after when William was asked to be the city recorder. I was surprised that he'd accepted such a big responsibility on top of his new job. I hoped it meant he was settling into town life, after mostly living on the farm. And, she nodded to Elvan, "I was right."

"I continued to get rides home from the Grange functions. One time, I took a big step of courage and invited William, his mother, and Rory to come for Sunday dinner. I'd already cleared it with Sarah with lots of promises that I would help do all the extra work. Sarah was gracious and easily complied.

"It didn't take much time for William and me to become fast friends. He seemed extremely interested in the library I was organizing and offered to build some shelves that I badly needed. Here he was, already a Sunday School teacher and city councilman, but he wanted to help me, and I was very touched by that. He loved teaching, his books, and his community.

"His most difficult job, currently, was being a city council member in Junction City. We'd been having a series of devastating fires set on purpose by an arsonist. But no one ever discovered who was doing such a terrible thing, destroying so many of our buildings and businesses. All the damage and monetary loss put added pressure on the townsfolk and the City Council. It was dreadfully discouraging for everyone in town. And, quite strangely, the churches and Grange Hall were never touched, and our schoolhouse was hit only once. Thank heavens, some men got there in time to prevent most of the school from burning.

"So, you see, in those scary times, the brightest spot in my week was seeing William Pitney and his little boy. But then, another tragedy soon hit us. Your great-grandmother, Elizabeth Pitney was turning 66, and both families and many friends gathered for a nice birthday celebration. But I remember some of the relatives whispering privately in the kitchen about Elizabeth's increased frailty.

"Just a month after that lovely party, a terrible thing happened. Mother Pitney went to town to visit some folks and ended up in our warehouse. I don't know why. We just know that when she leaned over a conveyor belt to shake hands and talk with a neighbor, Mr. Calvert, a corner of her knotted silk shawl got caught up in the moving machinery. She wasn't strong enough to resist and was pulled onto the belt and up to the silo before they could get the machines stopped. I can still feel the pain of that dreadful misfortune all these years later. I remember how ill and pale my father and Sarah looked for days. William appeared to be in shock and could hardly speak to anyone. I just hugged him for a long time and then he silently went home with Rory. What a terrible way to lose his mother! The whole town grieved this tragedy and many in the community gathered at the two churches that night to pray for the Pitneys. My family went to our Christian Church, all dressed in black, as I recall. William stayed home that night, or I gladly would have gone with him to his church. Of course, Papa completely shut down our granary for several days after that.

"Now, this terrible accident happened about eight months after William came to that first Sunday dinner with the Bushnells and Pitneys. William and I were very close now, so I often volunteered to help care for baby Rory because I could see that William and Melvina had their hands full with the funeral arrangements. The Pitney home was flooded with prepared meals, flowers and relatives coming into town. I think both families had a lot on their minds as they dealt with not only their feelings of loss, but also the circumstances around the accident. I remember that my father felt responsible because it happened in his warehouse, so he paid for the casket. The Pitneys turned out to be very compassionate people under these devasting conditions. They reassured our family that they considered it simply a tragic accident. William and Melvina both talked to my father and Sarah and stressed that in their minds it was their mother's feebleness that caused her death –and a bit of her own carelessness as well. They held firm to that and made sure that the rest of their siblings did not harbor any resentment, either. We Bushnells were so blessed by their attitude and appreciated our new friends even more. Or at least I did.

"Sarah always had a generous heart and often let me watch Rory in our home. Sometimes though, I took care of Royal at William's house. If he had some toys, he was a happy little boy.

"As life calmed down that year, it wasn't a surprise when, on Thanksgiving Day, William asked me to marry him. Ever since then Thanksgiving has always been an incredibly special day for me. We had a big church wedding on New Year's Day in 1879. Sarah and Father had never been able to put on a wedding before and we all three mightily enjoyed planning the happy event. I mean even your great grandfather Bushnell got into planning the festivities. My father especially loved a party and being with his friends!"

Elvan and Nettie both looked over as the store's front door opened and Jim and his folks exited and walked toward them. Jim climbed in the back again and handed Elvan a peppermint. Right before popping it into his mouth, Elvan stopped and told Jim, "Grandmother was telling me about how she met and married our grandpa. He sounds like a nice man."

As his mom and Dad settled into the front seat, Elvan asked one more question of his grandmother. "Did you get to go away for a honeymoon like the Neilsons are doing?"

Grandmother smiled and nodded to him. "Yes, dear. We took a three-day honeymoon to the beach at Yachats without little Royal, and then we came home to live in William's house. Before long we moved into my parents' house as they had built a new one just a block away. We had three more children of our own there: Your Aunt Nellie, Uncle Otis, and Uncle Cecil.

But your father, his younger sister and brother were born in another house on Birch Street."

Grandmother spoke a bit louder now so everyone could hear her. With a bit of pride in her voice she continued. "Anyway, while living in town, William ran the Bushnell warehouse, was city recorder, constable, owned the Hartford Fire Insurance Agency and was deputy tax assessor for the area. Then he was re-elected to the City Council and also began to serve on the school board. Plus, he was also president of the Lane County Pioneer Association and President of the Lane County Sunday School Union. That man loved public service and keeping busy!

Grandmother finished with, "It was a busy, but happy time for us," and gave Elvan a big grin. He smiled back and put the mint in his mouth.

# CHAPTER TWENTY-EIGHT

## *James and Sarah*

THE YEAR 1879 BECAME known to the locals as "the rusty year," on account of the wheat crop being almost totally destroyed by stem rust. The region had a very warm and wet spring followed by an equally warm and wet first part of Summer. This damp weather caused the wheat to grow exceptionally large and thick. Then just as the spring grain was in blossom, there came a few extremely hot and sultry days. The sudden heat seemed to burst the sap vessels in the stem and caused the grain to shrivel up. James' dismaying inspection of his fields determined that a great part of their spring wheat crop was now worthless. Sarah encouraged James to fight off his discouragement and look hopefully to their next crops. Their fall wheat still looked good, since it had been too far along to be injured much by the rust. That did help lessen James' worry.

What a wild winter Lane County endured! At the end of the year, on December 23, they had the coldest day on record. The thermometer hit seven degrees below zero. Then, January 9th brought the worst wind and rainstorm ever known in Oregon; counted in some places as a near hurricane.

Thankfully, a bright spot did appear in their lives on March 29. The First Christian Church of Junction City was organized. The first gospel message in the area occurred that year in the middle of George Bailey's field, due to James and this small congregation. Sarah was immensely proud when James was selected as the church's Elder. There were only eleven members at first. Even with both James and Sarah's stewardship, they could barely keep their young church alive. Over the next nine years, the church had several different preachers, found by the Bushnells who hired them and then kept them employed. That meant they paid the minister's salary with little help from the other church families. One Sunday a month, their Christian

Church was able to use the Cumberland Presbyterian Church. The rest of the time they continued to meet in the Grand Prairie schoolhouse. Finally, in 1881, they were able to construct a building of their own. However, it wasn't until 1889 that the church took on a new life and became stable without the Bushnells' financial help.

Harsh weather continued to plague the community and dishearten the farmers. The year of 1881 opened with wind and rainstorms, culminating in the highest flood waters in 20 years on January 4. All around the Bushnell's house, the muddy water was six to twelve inches deep. The flooding river ran strong throughout the town, washing away one-half of the sidewalks and a great deal of railroad tracks. The railroad trestles above and below town were completely washed away. That caused all communication with the outside world to be interrupted for what seemed like an endless amount of time. There whole valley rejoiced when the trains finally began running again. Sadly though, the town and its residents suffered severe hardships because of this flood that took years to overcome.

This was the second highest water mark the area had experienced since James came out west back in 1852. The first was the memorable flood of 1861–1862, spoken of as Noah's flood, when the lower part of the Willamette Valley was nearly all underwater. When rebuilding this time around 1881, the Oregon-California Railroad wisely raised their tracks. The railroad used the best known highwater mark and that flood record wasn't broken again in James' lifetime.

The original Junction City Christian Church

Once they got their house cleaned and the flood results under control, the household developed a pleasant rhythm again. Jennie and Olive, whom they called Ollie now, helped mind and care for their two little brothers while Sarah mostly nursed and tended to baby Mary. The two girls and the two younger boys, Henry and Walter, were going to the Junction City district school and learning very fast. Addie was old enough to care for himself most of the time, but not strong enough to do much outdoor work with James. His childhood back injury continued to cause his halting walk and currently, frequent pain.

All was joy and contentment in the busy Bushnell household, with Christmas coming soon. The little ones, especially, were happily looking forward to their Christmas.

But in the first week of December, Henry came home from school ill with diphtheria. James and Sarah didn't call the doctor but elected to treat Henry at home, where he was nursed back to health after this long and dangerous illness.

However, when Henry had been sick for about a week, eight-year-old Walter came down with the same dreaded disease. Even though this time James and Sarah immediately called the best doctors available to their home, Walter passed away on December 24th. On Christmas Day, they laid Walter's little body in the grave "to sleep until the last trumpet call," as James declared at the graveside.

After just one night of anguished rest, James and Sarah awoke the next morning to find their two-year-old angel, dear little Mary, violently ill. She was a sweet and patient sufferer, but the doctor said there was no hope for her recovery. This little one was unusually intelligent with a lovely disposition and endeared herself to everyone who got to know her. She died on the last day of the year in 1881 and on New Year's Day they had to lay her to rest beside her brother Walter.

Still, they had little time to grieve their two dear ones as now Addie, their crippled little warrior, began to demand all their attention when he was also stricken with diphtheria. Ever since his accident as a small boy while staying with his Aunt Helen, Addie's spinal injury had grown increasingly worse. After 15 years, he was almost doubled over and could hardly straighten himself at all. He also developed an awful ulcer in his groin that caused him much suffering and drained away his strength. Addie's diphtheria took his young life at age 16, a life filled with much anguish. Fourteen-year-old Ollie was the last to contract diphtheria, but only a light case. Thankfully, she survived.

Lucy Jennette arrived home from Monmouth in time to see her brother Addie before he died. They laid him alongside his mother and brothers and sisters — eight of his family who were already buried there. James was comforted by his unwavering faith that they were already "safe on the other shore and beholding the loving face of their heavenly Father for all eternity."

Brother G. M. Whitney of Eugene was an old family friend who'd preached at Charles' funeral service, back in 1874. Now he conducted another service for these three precious Bushnell children on February 16, 1882. He spoke from the text, "Suffer the little ones to come unto Me," the words of Jesus found in all four Gospels. Sarah and James both knew their well- loved children were safe in the arms of Jesus. Numbly they walked through those terrible grief-filled days with the hope that they would all be together again someday.

In the midst of their mourning, the weather also turned glum. It rained and rained. And it rained some more. Soon the river was again running forcefully through the heart of Junction City and was flooding the surrounding areas. On March 1st, they endured extremely high waters yet again. On March 18th and 19th, it snowed steadily all day long. Added on top of their grief, this dank weather made all the Bushnells feel too confined. To keep from brooding over the loss of their three children and the miserable weather, James and Sarah started planning a Spring trip to eastern Oregon and up into Washington with the remnant of their family. James wanted to visit their friends, the Henderson Murphy family, and see some beautiful country on the way.

# CHAPTER TWENTY-NINE

## *The Long Vacation*

THEY SELECTED THEIR LARGEST two-horse drawn wagon and fully packed it for camping. Then, they excitedly started their journey on the 23rd of June. They spent their first night at Soap Creek. They'd planned this first night close enough to home to serve as their trial run for camping out. This first night's trial helped them know just what they had forgotten at home. From Soap Creek, it wasn't far for James to go back. The next morning, he was tasked to return home and retrieve two more blankets and the larger spider pan for Sarah's camp cooking. Even with his round trip back to Junction City, which he did quickly on horse-back, they still reached Monmouth before noon the second day. Here they were joined by Sarah's sister-in-law and husband, the William Davidsons, and by all of Helen's family. After a satisfying visit, the Bushnells left Monmouth late in the afternoon and camped near Bethel. The following day they reached the Tualatin River at dark and, due to the late hour, had to camp on the riverbank surrounded by pigs and geese. The children were totally delighted with their animal companions that night!

They arrived in Portland by midday. James and Sarah marveled at how high the Willamette River was here, due to the backwater from the Columbia River. They took passage on The Wild West steamer with their wagon, team and all, and reached the Richmond House for their night's lodging, their one and only indoor accommodation on the entire trip. After getting the family back onboard the next morning with their wagon and team, James paid $37.25 for passage to The Dalles. They all sat on the upper deck watching the magnificent cliffs of the Columbia Gorge go by on both sides of the river. Henry was the first to spy a waterfall and soon they were all counting waterfalls as they passed by them on the Oregon side of the river.

Further along on this voyage, they had to transfer at the lower Cascades onto a smaller boat. They got off the smaller boat at the foot of the upper Cascades and watched as their wagon was hauled around the falls over onto the Washington side. Most all the other passengers were also intrigued by the maneuvering around these falls and were watching, too. There they boarded "The Queen of the West" steamer and reached The Dalles at 7:30 that evening. They were pleasantly surprised to see Sarah's Uncle and Aunt Montgomery, and their friend Henderson Murphy, all gathered there to greet them. After some happy visiting, the Bushnells camped for the night among many rocks, sand banks, and thistles along The Dalles riverbank.

The following day, the whole group crossed the Columbia and drove about five miles to the Narrows, where the Indians were catching their winter's supply of salmon. Here the mighty river compressed into a channel so steep and narrow that it seemed to be just a stone's throw across it. The Indians were camping on the rocks with their families in large numbers. The Bushnells and their friends watched fascinated as the Indians fished from the rocks by dipping nets into the roiling water. As soon as one netted a salmon, the women took the fish and quickly and neatly removed the bones. Then the split fish was laid on the rocks in the sun until it cured. Once dried, it would be rubbed into small, fine pieces, neatly wrapped in bark cloth, and packed up for their journey back to their winter camp. Henderson said the salmon were an important part of the tribes' yearly food supply.

After the fun of catching a few of their own salmon, the Bushnells left their fish for the Montgomerys. Leaving in the late afternoon, the Bushnells and Mr. Murphy camped halfway up on a high mountain ten miles from The Dalles. They visited Goldendale the next day, which they thought was a pretty little town surrounded by immense open country. They had dinner the following day in Hock Creek Canyon, a deep rocky gulch with some fine-looking peach orchards. Curious about the view, they climbed some four miles up a mountain, until they reached the top. The amazing view here encompassed miles of country from The Dalles and Cascade Mountains on the west to the Blue Mountains on the east, a vast expanse without a house or green tree in sight. There were trees down below in the gulches, but out of sight. The country here was an immense sand plain with the sand sculpted into ridges by the western wind. Nearly all the area was dotted with patches of ground where the soil had been blown away to a depth of two or three feet, leaving nothing but rock or clay. The farmers called it scab land. It didn't look very fertile.

They reached the home of Henderson Murphy late in the evening. The Murphy family lived in a shack on a little creek, which surprised all the Bushnells, but probably little Henry the most. Sarah had to "hush" him several times, to not insult their friends and hosts. Mrs. Murphy explained this was their summer cabin. They had a good garden and a few acres of grain but were mostly sheep farmers. The first day there it rained in torrents and the rain came through the cabin roof in sheets for a while. Again, Henry started to complain, but this time his sister Helen quickly scolded him to keep quiet.

The Bushnell and Murphy families traveled to the foothills near Bickleton, an unincorporated community in Klickitat County, Washington, for a Fourth of July celebration. No one appeared to know exactly where it was to be held, and after quite a bit of looking, a group of the searchers decided to just stop, join together and celebrate. They all had a fine celebration in that make-do way.

On the fifth, Mr. Murphy took them to an Indian camp to buy an un-broken, wild pony for their trip. The Indians had collected a whole band of horses that had not yet been tamed or broken. One Indian threw a lariat over the head of a painted pony and wrapped the rope around a limb of a fallen tree. The horse did some furious kicking and jumping, but as the slack in the rope was all taken up, the horse's head was eventually close enough to the limb for an Indian man to slip a strong halter over his head. Much to James' surprise, Mr. Murphy tied that halter to the tail of his own pony, mounted his pony and started off for home. James had never seen such bucking and wild cavorting that went on next! Sometimes the wild stallion even threw himself flat on his side. However, whether standing or lying, the horse was being dragged along by Mr. Murphy's horse. Although a smaller animal, the lead horse sometimes dragged the wild one on an upgrade of as much as 15 or 20 feet. The Bushnells were amazed. Before they had gotten back to the Murphy home, that wild horse was following the lead horse quite obediently.

The Bushnells reluctantly waved goodbye to the Murphy family after a few more days and traveled over the rolling prairie country, descending to the Columbia River across from Arlington, Oregon. They were ferried across the wide and fast-moving river on a flat boat propelled by two fellows on oars. It took them all afternoon to cross because of the strong current. Whenever they neared a set of rapids, Sarah insisted that all the children move close to the wagon and keep a tight hold. She even set Henry, the youngest, inside it. He protested some, but all the children obeyed her.

Once done with that long and dangerous crossing, they camped on the east bank of a stream. Here they experienced their first sandstorm, and although they crawled into the tent and fastened everything down tightly, they were soon covered with sand an inch deep. They slept the best they could with the blowing sand in their blankets, noses and even mouths. They all complained about the grit in their teeth. Before they could get started in the morning, they had to spend time shaking and slapping the sand out of all their bedding. Most of the family took off their outer clothes and shook them too. That didn't remove all the sand, but it was the best they could do.

On July 14, they reached Willow Springs and later crossed the John Day River headed for Prineville. They saw no inhabitants from Arlington to Grass Valley—five days of traveling. There was little water except for an occasional spring. In Bake Oven, they were thrilled to find a beautiful spring of clear, chilly water. James thought this was an exceptionally beautiful portion of the country with fine grass and water. From the locals, they learned that this land seemed to be attracting emigrants from California, who were settling into the area that summer, also.

One of the most remarkable sights they discovered was Buckhorn Canyon. James had been driving their wagon along over a seemingly flat prairie without any bush or tree in sight. The road took a dip into a little depression and kept going down for a mile or more to a beautiful little creek. Its banks were lined with trees and underbrush, a perfect oasis in the barren land. They happily camped there. The next day the horses pulled them back up the steep ascent to level ground again. As luck would have it, they were soon struck by an army of grasshoppers. Millions upon millions of them crawled on the ground, one or two inches deep. Their clicking and whirring noise was all anyone could hear without shouting close to another person's ear. The sky was so full of them that it looked like a heavy snowstorm. Everyone hated the critters, but it was Sarah and the small children who stayed hidden and covered up inside their wagon. James and the boys were tasked with knocking the grasshoppers off the wagon bed before they could crawl inside. That kept them terribly busy! On the ground outside their wagon, there was not a green thing left anywhere after the hungry hoard passed. The devastation was sobering. Ollie said it well enough for all of them. "I never, ever want to go through that again as long as I live!"

They arrived at Prineville the next day a little before dark and stayed the night with James' nephew, John Bushnell. The next morning, they departed his family and headed west, toward home. Getting travel-weary, James and Sarah were determined to head straight home, and by the fastest route. They reached the Deschutes River by nightfall and found dry, arid country without timber on either side of the river. They passed through high rolling hills and more barren looking country covered with a scattering of tamarack trees. They found a camping spot at the foot of the mountains and took dinner at nearby Squaw Creek, where they drank of the crystal waters coming right from the melting ice and snow.

They ascended the Ochoco Mountains the next day. Near the summit, they passed the extinct crater of a volcano that was about 100 feet in depth, with trees growing on its inner sides. The caldera still showed traces of volcanic action. Going down a long, sandy mountain trail, they came to some lava beds. This large tract was entirely covered with lava, full of holes and crevasses over and around where the road ran. James could imagine how frightful this place would have been back when it was a mass of melted and boiling lava.

The family camped that night at Fish Lake at the head waters of the McKenzie River, which ran nearly south from there. All around them stood the finest of timber: fir, pine, and cedar. A quarter of a mile farther was Clear Lake, which Glenn and Ollie explored. They understood how it got its name as they came back to describe the exceeding transparency of its water. The rest of the family decided it was worth the extra walk to see this beautiful spot. Once the Bushnells were all in sight of the lake, they stood and stared at the clear beauty. It was Glenn who pointed out how the old crater was filled with a forest of trees, still standing below the surface of the water.

Leaving their camp at Fish Lake, they slowly descended a seven-mile hill. After camping a night on the Santiam River, they followed it down to the Upper Soda and Soda Springs. Seeing the bubbling springs, little Henry was intrigued and curious. He asked over and over if he could taste the delicious-looking water. Finally, James agreed that anyone who wanted to, could taste it. Just one swallow and the little lad was satisfied. "Yuck. It looks good. It tastes awful!" His parents laughed, and his older siblings were now more hesitant. They did try it, though, and agreed with Henry.

Soon, the family drove through the village of Sweet Home. From there, they followed the Calapooya River to the Willamette Valley, which James declared was the most beautiful spot he'd seen on their entire journey!

# CHAPTER THIRTY

*Home Again*

WHEN THEY ARRIVED HOME on August 1, 1882, everything was found to be as it should. They'd been gone for one month and a day. Sarah began the unpacking and reorganizing of their household. She hummed along as she worked. She was glad to be home again. The trip's beautiful change of scenery had been uplifting, but the journey had also been tiring for her. Keeping a family fed and happy while traveling and camping so much wasn't easy. James immediately got busy cleaning and preparing the warehouse, because they would soon be taking in lots of grain once again. The sightseeing trip had helped, and life was looking better for both of them.

In the fall, it rained hard for a week and was so warm that the snow melted in the mountains, causing the Willamette River to rise to flood levels and run swiftly through the town. Again. After that, a blizzard surged up the valley, turning it cold very quickly. Unusually cold. One morning the thermometer read 18 degrees. It dropped to nine on the following day and held at six degrees for the next two days. The sun shone clear and pleasant during the day and the sloughs, ponds and ditches were covered with ice. It made splendid ice skating for the boys and girls.

This unusual weather, with the alternating freezing and thawing, killed nearly every blade of the growing winter wheat. James and many others had to depend on their spring wheat reserves, but some of the younger farmers had to go to California for seed to resow all their fields.

## ANOTHER CHILD

On March 15, 1883, Sarah and James greeted another little girl whom they named Gertrude. It was a peaceful and pleasant spell in their lives. Already

in late March, farmers were nearly done seeding, home gardens were partially laid, fruit trees were in blossom, and it looked and felt like May.

The next month, James left Sarah and their newborn in the willing
hands of their family and headed to Portland. He knew Nettie and William
would help Sarah if she needed it. He was off in search of an evangelist for
the Lane County Board of Churches, of which he was President. He went as
far as Corvallis by stagecoach and spent the night with Rev. Bruce Wolver-
ton, who preached and pastored the church there, and was also Secretary
of the State Board. James traveled on to Monmouth the next day to visit his
sister Helen and her family. He stayed with them for two nights, visiting
the college and admiring the new business growth surrounding the school.
Then he went on to Portland where he found Brother Wiltse, an evangelist
and preacher, who had just arrived from the East. James brought Rev. Wiltse
home with him, and Wiltse proved to be an excellent preacher. He did some
admirable work in the county as an evangelist, preaching for over a year in
Junction City.

## IMPROVING TOWN LIFE

While in Monmouth, and later in southwest Portland, James had become
intrigued and studied the water systems of both communities. He shared
with Sarah his new thoughts regarding how Junction City could profit from
its own water supply. She thought it was a promising idea, too. He wrote to
Monmouth's mayor for information. After studying the Monmouth plans
and documents, he felt ready to tackle the job.

George Boyd was contacted to dig the well. Boyd was digging down
a considerable distance on a sweltering day, when a friend came by with a
cold bottle of beer. "Come on up and have a drink with me, George."

George climbed up and had just reached the top, when the well caved
in completely! It was quite a shock to both men, as they stood looking down
at the collapsed timbers and remaining hole. George Boyd spoke first and
grinned, saying "I'm sure glad I'm not a tea-totaler. That bottle there just
saved my life!"

Once the well was dug out again, James enlisted the help of two Pitneys: Royal and William, and in 1891, they completed the first water system
in Junction City. It consisted of two metal water tanks placed on top of his
own warehouse along East 4th Avenue. The two tanks held 5,000 and 6,000
gallons each and were filled using a large squeaky windmill. The windmill
stood at 110 feet tall. City rates for water were $10 for the first faucet and
$19 for two, and that was the limit per household or business. Soon, James

established a ten-year contract to furnish the Southern Pacific Railroad Company with water.

James hired his 14-year-old grandson, Royal, to keep the windmill and water running. The constant racket from the windmill drew many complaints from the neighbors. Consequently, the neighbors and the whole community were very relieved when James finally replaced the noisy windmill with a steam engine to pump the water.

James was re-elected to the City Council while the need for sidewalks was still being debated at the general meetings in the Spring of 1892. The town's frequent flooding and the Willamette Valley's rainy climate in general, made for very muddy streets.

Soon after one of these meetings, James and Sarah eagerly awaited a visit from Ollie, who'd married a railroad man, Walter Beebe. A few years before, his work had taken the young couple south to live in Ashland. Walter's railroad job allowed the Bushnells to enjoy free train passes. Those passes meant that they were able to have regular visits with their dear grandson Henry, now a year old, and his parents. Ollie and Walter hadn't been able to make it back home the for Christmas, and the Bushnells were greatly anticipating this visit. It would be just Ollie and little Henry on this trip, and Sarah had hardly talked of anything else since they'd received the previous week's telegram.

It was near dark and close to dinnertime, when Sarah and James walked the few blocks over to the station. Anticipating the train's arrival, all the siblings, of course, wanted to greet their big sister and tagged along with their parents. The day's heavy rain had let up and was now only drizzling lightly. The train pulled in right on time. When the screeching brakes finally quit, Ollie stood on the steps one car ahead of them, waving and shouting. Disembarking with her toddler in her arms, she didn't wait for her family to reach her. She didn't wait for any assistance, but just took the steps down in quick succession. However, the family saw her stagger slightly with her precious load, then slip off the bottom step. She landed solidly on both feet, plopping onto the muddy street with a huge splash and Ollie's astonished cry. The muddy water splashed up on Ollie's coat and even splattered the corner of little Henry's favorite baby blue knit blanket, which had been hanging down low. In a single unhappy shout, Sarah wailed, "No, not the baby blanket!" as Ollie cried, "No, I just cleaned this coat!" After regaining her balance, Ollie lifted her beige calf-leather boots high with each step and met her mother and stepfather's open arms. She quickly handed over little Henry and checked out the muddy splotches on her boots and outfit. "Father, when is Junction City ever going to get sidewalks?" she wailed. "This is the only town on my whole route today that requires passengers to get out in the mud. And you are on the City Council, so I've heard. It's ridiculous to be so far behind the other towns!" Sarah decided to calm her daughter down by changing the subject, which wasn't hard with darling little Henry in her arms. They hadn't seen him for four months, and Sarah noisily "oohed" and "ahhed" over Henry so that everyone, including Ollie, chuckled at the grandmother's delight. Now chatting more happily, the family all took off toward home.

James had heard enough, though! Soon after that incident, the town got its wooden sidewalks. Due to the frequent flooding, the city's new boardwalk was constructed above the street on each block at the railroad's high-water mark. At each intersection, it sloped back down to street level where the sidewalk continued across the street on bare ground again. Then, back up it went, out of the flood zone, for the next block until the next street corner. Then, back down it sloped again. This seemed to be the only way to keep the sidewalks from flooding every year. The new, mostly dry, sidewalks pleased the locals and the travelers alike. James was quite proud of his city's big improvements.

Sad news arrived from California. William, the brother James had miraculously found in the hills of California during his first gold mining trip, now lived in San Francisco. The Bushnells learned by post that William had died on April 29, 1885, suffering a sudden attack of bowel dysfunction. His sickness was short and painful. James had not seen him for several years and now greatly regretted that. He and Sarah wrote a long overdue letter to William's wife, Maria, and the three sons William left behind: Waters, Arthur and R. Edward. The last James knew, all still resided and worked in the San Francisco area.

In July 1888, there was more sad news. Edward Adkins, James' good friend and brother-in-law (husband of his sister Helen), died of a large tumor. The newspaper reported: "He'd suffered untold horrors with it before death came to his release." James reached Monmouth in time to observe the autopsy performed by Dr. L.L. Rowland of Salem. They discovered that the tumor was as large as a good-sized hen's egg. This was the only autopsy James had ever attended. After witnessing this one, he decided that he needn't ever see one again!

The Fourth of July celebration in the grove was a bright spot in 1888, with a great crowd in attendance, generally all having an enjoyable time. Because he was serving as Mayor for another term, James was delighted to preside over the patriotic gathering.

# CHAPTER THIRTY-ONE

## *Becoming a "Civilized Town"*

ONCE AGAIN JAMES HAD the building bug. He'd enjoyed great satisfaction after adding the water towers and sidewalks for Junction City and was seeking a new project. James and Sarah had frequently discussed the sparse cultural offerings in their small, beloved town. Even Eugene didn't have much to offer as refined entertainment. Sarah's family, the Davidsons, had kindled in her a love for music and enjoyment of the theatre. Moving to Junction City, she had gladly forgone these passions for marriage to a farmer and motherhood. And that had kept her plenty busy! But now that their children were grown and Sarah was a townswoman, she was increasingly missing the fine arts. She complained that Salem or Oregon City were the closest cities to go to hear a concert, and both were such long all-day trips. She started dreaming of what they could build in Junction City to bring cultural events right here to them. Her dreaming caught James' attention, and together they began plotting exciting additions to their hometown.

Then they built, according to their well-thought-out plans. First Sarah and James constructed the Junction City Hotel on Front Street, a brick building occupying about a half block and costing them $20,000. Instead of importing bricks, they used bricks from the local clay pits. A brickyard had been started east of town, and the red-orange bricks made for an impressive look. Next, their new block grew to include several retail stores: the G.S. Keck Barber Shop, Mrs. Sibbet's Millinery, S.P. Gilmore General Merchandise, and the C.F. Hulburt Store. Then, they added a ballroom that soon hosted many town events.

Henry was dating a local girl at the time. Sarah convinced her teenaged son that any girl would appreciate a man who could dance, so he reluctantly started weekly dance lessons at the ballroom. Soon, he was reveling in the extra attention he was getting from many girls who were also taking lessons. Being taller than both his parents, Henry's lanky awkwardness evened out with the dance practice, too. When live bands started playing at the weekly dances, his reluctance completely disappeared. He even thanked his mother for her good advice! The first girlfriend didn't last through his new-found popularity, though. He was now enjoying what he called "playing the field."

One day, his little sister Gertrude told Sarah that she'd heard one of Henry's girlfriends crying at school, because Henry had promised another girl his first and last dance on Friday. It was obvious that Gertie relished tattling on her older brother and his many girlfriends, and Sarah tried to act uninterested in front of her young daughter. However, she did feel quite badly for the heartbroken schoolgirl, whose mother was one of Sarah's good friends.

Sarah spoke to James about it one night. "I'm not sure Henry is being careful with all these girls' feelings. He seems to be encouraging all their attention, and I know that will make for some hurt feelings. What has happened to our sweet son, James?"

James looked at her over his newspaper and replied, "I think he'll learn not to spread himself too thin. Although, it may take a strong young lady to set him straight; or a truly bad experience for him to learn by. Don't worry too much. He's only 17."

Henry went on to enjoy his popularity for two more years in high school and then graduated with his class in the very ballroom his parents had built. He went on to Monmouth Normal School, as it was now called, just like his older siblings, but later came back and married the same girl whom Gertie heard crying that day at school.

After the ballroom, the next development was a large and magnificent 5,000 sq. ft. Opera House that James built with hired help. All the Bushnells' new structures were partially constructed of the same clay brick, with fire such a constant threat to the community.

The Opera House offered a nice variety of concerts. James and Sarah began bringing in bands and orchestras from all over the western states. Sarah preferred classical music, but James countered that they needed a variety for all types of music lovers. Plus, he liked to believe that they were helping to educate younger people to appreciate many styles of music, not just the classics. Next, the Bushnells booked stage performances that were touring along the west coast. It took quite a bit of work to recruit and bring these groups to their new establishment, but they both thrived on the challenge. Sarah still had some connections through her Davidson relatives, which helped. The Opera House was able to lure famous shows such as "Uncle Tom's Cabin." In addition, many civic events, including school graduation ceremonies, were held there annually. Within four years, one newspaper declared their Junction City Opera House to be "the finest between Seattle and San Francisco."

On May 2, 1893, James helped open the Farmers and Merchants Bank, along with the other directors C.W. Washburne, J.P. Milliorn T.A. Milliorn, and George Pickett. James was the bank president until his death, and he and Sarah invested a lot of their money there. The bank was usually called the Washburne Bank by local folks, because three generations of Washburnes cashiered there.

**Ballroom and Opera House block**

**Farmers and Merchants Bank**

# CHAPTER THIRTY-TWO

## *Elvan McClure Pitney, age 13*

ONE DAY AFTER SCHOOL, Elvan took his glass of milk, an apple, and a piece of bread into the dining room to sit near his grandmother. She was wrapped in a blanket in the rocking chair close to the fire with her feet on a stool. He knew she was usually cold, no matter where she sat or what time of day it was. She smiled at him, said "hello," and kept rocking. He often wondered what she was thinking when she rocked in her chair—especially right now, because she suddenly chuckled out loud!

"Grandmother, what are you thinking about that's so funny?" He wanted to know.

"Well, it's that funny thing your grandfather did in the spring he bought the bear cubs. Actually, I think your father would have been about your age when it happened."

"Please tell it to me again. I haven't heard that story since I was little," Elvan almost begged.

"Well, it is quite a story! It all started with a trapper and his bear cubs who were traveling down the Pacific Coast Road. Your grandfather and I were there visiting his cousins in Yaquina Bay. The cubs were giving the man quite a bit of trouble and slowing down his travels too much. So, he asked your grandfather, William, if he wanted to buy them from him. I will never understand why, but Will took a liking to those bear cubs. He bought them right up without ever asking me. Your Uncle Marcellus had to truck them home for us. Then, William kept them chained out under the big oak tree most of the time. I insisted that he keep them chained up. Pretty soon, though, he let the cubs loose to see what they would do. They loved exploring our land leading with their noses. Mostly, though, it turned out that they just followed your grandfather around like puppies. One cub stopped eating and quit playing and eventually died, even though we tried our hardest to keep it alive.

"First, our children learned to keep away from them, because there were only really calm with William. Whenever anyone else came too near, the cubs got nervous. The surviving one still followed your grandpa around just as much as ever. When one of the children tried to get near it, it would stop, look at them, and struggle to stand up. Then it roared its little roar. It made us all laugh at such valiant efforts!

"Will eventually enjoyed walking all over the farm with that cub following him. Then, it began to show interest in the children. It started to playfully chase them and even took to playing hide-and-seek with them. The children would do the hiding and the bear never gave up until it had found all of them. The boys learned to swim in Bryant Lake by hanging onto the cub's back. It was quite a family pet. I even liked that little cub, except for all the times it got into our sugar barrel on the back porch. Then, it wasn't worth the mess it made for me.

"I could put up with having a pet bear on our farm, but I was really embarrassed, when William started taking it into town with him in the wagon! I always thought he was way too proud of that cub. It quickly grew large, yet Will didn't seem to care and still took it into town with him on its chain.

"Anyway, one day in Junction City, he and his cub walked by a group of miners fresh from Florence gold mines sitting around on the sidewalk. They all got a big laugh at the bear following William around, and one of them, Kit Baker, yelled out, "I bet my dog could sure whip that bear!" Well, for some reason that I'll never figure out, Will took him up on it. No one had much money in those days, but there were some good wagers placed on the match. Kit himself bet $100 on his dog whipping the Pitney bear. The odds favored that fellow's dog, because it did have some fighting experience and looked really mean. The bear was still so young and tame.

"The two men set a time a few days later for the fight. Will cleared out a part of the Bushnell sack warehouse, a spacious area by the main elevator. He had to make room, for a big crowd was expected to come watch. That evening, it seemed like most of the men of the town came. William and the bear waited inside the center until the man brought in his dog. The doors were locked. Then, Kit immediately said "sic 'em" to his dog, and it attacked from the bear's rear. At first the cub thought the dog was just playing and he responded back as in play, which made everyone pretty convinced the dog was going to win. However, after the dog had nipped the bear fiercely a few times, it began to get mad. It turned on the dog and now started in earnest chasing the dog all through the crowd. Everyone laughed and cheered. Tired of being bitten again, the bear caught up with the dog and gave it a solid smack to the side of its head. At this, the dog let out a yelp, turned tail and ran to the door, clawing to clear out of that place.

"Well, Elvan, all the men betting on the dog had to pay your grandfather. He made quite a few dollars, but mostly he was prouder of that bear than ever before. However, after a while, the bear became more unruly and hard for even William to handle. It was an extremely hard decision when he decided he needed to sell it. The circus came through town that fall, and they bought our bear."

His grandmother hadn't even paused once as she told this story, and Elvan had stopped chewing. Now, he closed his gaping mouth and said, "I can hardly believe all this is true. I've never heard about this fight before, and I can't believe about the betting. I thought Pitneys weren't allowed to make bets. That's what Jim and I are always told."

She replied, "This story is definitely all true, although I am sorry those bets were made. It was mere foolishness and pride that took ahold of William—two of the very things that God doesn't like. Do as you've been told, Elvan, as it's the best way."

At dinner that night, Elvan couldn't wait to bring up the bear cub story. First, he watched his family eat their ham and green beans. Then when his dad started buttering his bread, he spoke up. He began with, "The story about the bear and dog fight was interesting when Grandmother told it to me today." His mother and father paused in their eating and exchanged a glance. He went on, "It didn't sound like the Pitneys at all, because it was very exciting and there was a lot of betting for money going on. How come I didn't hear about that dog and bear fight before? Did you know about it, Jim?"

His older brother stared questioningly at Elvan, then stopped shoveling his fork. He shrugged and said, "I only know what Jimmy Brown told me, and that's from what his dad told him. That was a long time ago, too. How come we didn't hear about it?"

In response to both boys' questions, the two Pitney adults all turned their heads slowly towards Ellen, the boys' mother. She didn't smile, but solemnly nodded, saying, "That's because I think it's the most foolish thing I'd ever heard. I don't want to ever put such nonsense in the head of my young boys. In my opinion, it's certainly nothing to be proud of."

Their father turned from their mother and just stared into his plate. Soon, though, he raised his eyes to look at Elvan. With a big wink and slight grin, he said, "And there you have it, son."

Their dinner was very quiet after that.

# CHAPTER THIRTY-THREE

## *James Begins Another New Venture*

### AUGUST 1895

WHEN JAMES REMINISCED BACK to the time when he was a young, new settler, he never forgot how he and Elisabeth had been richly blessed by the generosity of the Briggs family. Now in his mature years, James never missed an opportunity to pass on this good example of generosity. It gave him immense pleasure to help in the lives of his family and his community. He gave his time and energy freely to others and used his money to help when needed.

Ever since settling in the Willamette Valley, James had avidly supported bringing new preachers out to the west. He had been quick to recognize the shortage of good ministers in their young Oregon communities and used his means to bring many divinity school graduates from back east to churches in Alvadore, Grand Prairie, Junction City, and other surrounding areas.

Now 40 some years later, he was still concerned with the very same need: more preachers in the Willamette Valley and all throughout the west. At first, only Sarah and a few of his family knew he was dreaming about starting a Bible school. In his dreams, this school would prepare young people for church ministry in the Valley. Then, over the next two years he'd started expressing his vision at the Annual Convention of the Christian Church in Turner. More recently, he'd discussed the need at the Oregon State Missionary Board meeting where he was Vice-President. In all this talk, he found a few men at each meeting that truly heard him and understood his passion. It took a while, but eventually others became enthusiastic, too.

Then his life changed after one such conversation with Eugene Sanderson, the current pastor of the biggest Christian Church in Oregon. James was immediately attracted to the younger man. Brother Sanderson's strong heart for the Lord's work and strong educational background made quite an impression on James. Sanderson had moved out West after attaining his bachelor's and master's degrees in arts and attending one additional year at Yale Divinity School. James returned home to Sarah extolling the abilities of this man. He'd just found a new partner and visionary for starting a Bible school!

One fine July day in 1895, James walked into town to get the mail and visit with the men idling around the porch at City Hall. This was his number- one daily pleasure. It was also the biggest reason he and Sarah planned to spend the rest of their lives living in town. After the weather, the crops, and their health were thoroughly discussed by the friends, James stood and excused himself by saying that Sarah expected some help paring apples for her pies and he'd best get going. But first he stopped by the Post Office. Sarah teased him relentlessly if he forgot his original errand before coming home, as he often did.

Glancing through their mail—after only a ten-minute conversation with Postmaster Isaac Senders — he stopped his sorting when he came to the official looking letter coming from E. C. Sanderson. He quickened his pace down Front Street and on to home. Just as he'd predicted, when he strode through the kitchen door, he saw that Sarah had already started peeling the apples.

She smiled at him and asked about the mail.

"You've got a letter from Jennie, and I've got something interesting from E.C. Sanderson. Do you want your letter now, or after you're done with the apples?"

Sarah looked at the apples and looked at the letter he was holding. "Hand me the letter, please. These apples can wait and then you'll be able to help me later." She smiled her sweetest smile at him, and he chuckled back at her.

After he handed her Jennie's letter, James sat down in the kitchen rocking chair and pulled out his pocketknife. He carefully slit the top of the envelope, closed his pocketknife and put it back in his pocket before he pulled out the letter. He unfolded it with care and mused aloud, "I hope this is a follow-up to our latest discussion about the Bible school. There was strong agreement at last month's meeting, as you know, dear. We all determined it was God's will for us to get it started as soon as we could."

And sure enough, the letter from Eugene Sanderson was calling a meeting to plan the startup of a Bible school in the city of Eugene. When the date arrived, James eagerly attended with Sarah and Brother Skaggs from their church. Sarah was happy to see Prudence Sanderson also in attendance. Knowledgeable through experience, both women reasoned that they should be a part of their husbands' undertakings. Sarah, especially, because of her husband's age.

At that meeting, it was determined that the school's purpose would be to educate and prepare young men and women for the ministry. The matter had previously been thoroughly discussed and was very favorably received at this meeting. Eugene Sanderson, being younger than James, was willing to do the bulk of the work. Because of his belief that locating ministerial schools near public colleges and universities provided the best of both worlds, Sanderson wanted to open their new school close to the University of Oregon. That way, the Bible students could get a liberal arts degree while also focusing on courses in theology, the Bible, oratory, and music. Having just recently returned from a trip to the Midwest, Sanderson had added several more degrees to his already impressive resume: another bachelor's degree, this time in Divinity; a Doctor of Law from Drake University; plus, a Bachelor of Sacred Theology from the University of Chicago. In James' mind, this outstanding academic background made Sanderson well-equipped to be the school's first and only teacher and its dean, at least at the beginning.

Sanderson's unique proposal was quickly endorsed by all. There were no other schools in the West like this, with an emphasis on Divinity study. Next, the new school's founders appointed a committee to canvas the town for the start-up funding to launch the school. The funding committee's report was soon favorable, so the school was organized as The Eugene Divinity School. A Board of Regents was elected: J. W. Coles, W. H. Osburne, J. H. Hawley, J. D. Matlock, J. T. Callison, J. P. Flint, and James A. Bushnell. Sixty-nine-year-old James was elected president of the Regents.

James was so excited about the upcoming birth of the college that it was all he could talk about when he and Sarah got home to Junction City. He proclaimed to Sarah and others, "What a precious gift from God was that long-ago day when Eugene Sanderson came west to pastor churches here!"

James contributed to their new mission with finances, much of the planning, and constant prayer. He also added his personal zeal, recruiting other Christian men to support the school with their finances and prayers. He always said that every contribution, no matter what size, was just as important as another.

The Divinity school opened later that year, on October 15, 1895, in a rented room one block from the University of Oregon. That first Fall there were five students, all taking connected studies at the University across the street. The founders strongly believed that the school would grow and fulfill the great mission of supplying Gospel preachers for the entire West Coast of the United States.

Sarah declared that James acted just like the father of a new baby—he was that proud.

## JULY 27, 1901

His family joyfully celebrated James' 75th birthday with all his children and grandchildren within reach coming together. Sarah happily played hostess, with the tables set up beneath the oak trees. The 16 Bushnells enjoyed a very pleasant time together. James reminisced, looking back over the year, and expressed gratefulness "to his Heavenly Father for His kind care and guiding hand which had led him along all his years." He thanked God for giving him a good degree of health and strength and for how good he still felt at age 75.

In the spring of 1902, Sarah was amazed by the numerous large bands of migratory sandhill cranes. She wrote to Ollie "that these beautiful gray birds stand about three feet high and have a vibrant, two-tone trill. When they're done feeding, the most unusual sight happens. They rise almost perpendicularly by circling up and around in circles of several hundred yards width. This circling creates a vacuum, and they spiral upward like this for several hours before they are completely out of sight. It is amazing to behold."

The cranes stopped coming after a few years, and Sarah, plus the whole community, missed the springtime visitors after that.

James, Sarah, and their daughter Gertrude went to the annual Turner Convention together. They were delighted with the largest attendance they had ever had and best meetings they could remember. The attendance was enormous: estimated at 6,000 to 7,000. The Bushnells had attended this annual convention of the Christian Church for a great many years, and each one had been a source of great inspiration to James. He particularly enjoyed meeting with his brothers and sisters in Christ from all over Oregon, renewing old acquaintances and making new ones. He found this fellowship always strengthened him for any spiritual conflicts he might meet in the next year, due to all his responsibilities. For the fifth year in a row, James was elected vice president of the Christian Missionary Society. Ten days later, James and Sarah reached home again and found all was well.

On July 27, James met the 76th milestone of his life's journey. Although he still enjoyed a good degree of health, he admitted to Sarah that he felt more and more like an old man, especially when the thermometer reached 95 degrees two or three times that same week. Sarah responded that he certainly didn't ever act like an old man and had more energy than most men ten years younger than him!

# CHAPTER THIRTY-FOUR

## June 28, 1903

THE BUSHNELLS AND NEIGHBORS enjoyed a dry spell of weather, after a very cool spring. They were still feeling the warm contentment that they always felt after arriving back home from Turner. It was another one of the very best annual conventions ever held. Brother Allen Wilson, considered one of the Christian Church's foremost evangelists, did most of the preaching. While still at home, James had talked with Sarah about going off the Mission Board. Sarah, in turn, had shocked daughter Gertrude when she whispered, "I can bet money that isn't going to happen." James did resign, but instead was re-elected vice president of the Oregon Christian Missionary Convention for the sixth time!

He also continued as President of the Board of Regents of the Eugene Divinity School for his eighth year. In town, James was serving on the boards of the Junction City Hotel Company for his twelfth year and the Farmers and Merchants Bank for eleven years.

He turned 77 on July 27th and was beginning to grow a little weary from these responsibilities. He spent the day quietly at home, contemplating the recent years of his pilgrimage on earth. He was still operating his warehouse, but with nowhere near the amount of grain he once processed. Local farmers were raising more stock cattle, sheep, and hogs, and turning their wheat fields into dairy farms. Also, with an increasing population, the mill was using more wheat and storing less.

On January 1, 1904, James added to his diary: "Another year has gone to join the many pasts and is lost to the great ocean of Eternity. Lost? No, verily nothing is lost. It is only blended in the great throng of years which go to make up the onward march until suns shall cease to roll and God's angel shall stand and declare the edict of the Creator. Time was, time is, but time shall be no more."

He attended a meeting of the State Missionary Board in Eugene and was pleased to find that the work had greatly expanded during the year, with some $2,300 raised and expended in spreading the Gospel through the state. Afterward, he commented, "It is a blessed work the Board is doing, and I like the situation, but think on account of my increasing deafness, I shall lay down the work at Turner next June."

This time Sarah boldly replied to him, "That will never happen." And the next year, she was right!

After a pleasant winter, James went to Eugene to attend the Divinity School's Commencement on May 28 and the annual meeting of the Board of Regents in the afternoon. The school was prosperous and growing. Best of all, they were out of debt and had established a good beginning for an endowment fund of several thousand dollars. Forty full-time students attended that spring. James was elected Regent again for a three-year term and elected president for another year. He had continually held the office of President since the founding of the school.

At the following year's Commencement in 1904, Brother M.L. Rose from Tacoma preached the Baccalaureate sermon. Following which James enthusiastically assisted ordaining three young men and one woman to the ministry by praying and laying on of hands.

# CHAPTER THIRTY-FIVE

*Visiting Idaho, Yellowstone*
*National Park, and the former*
*World's Fair sights in One Trip*

IN THE SUMMER OF 1906, the voters in Oregon had a chance to say whether they wanted "the open saloon" in their communities. James and Sarah were against the ballot measure and believed alcohol to be the cause of more than half the crime and misery in the country. This June 4th election would decide whether the state's towns would have local options to serve alcohol. The state vote was affirmative by a large majority. The Bushnells were extremely disappointed, but still hoped that their own Lane County, at least, would vote out alcohol on the November 1906 Presidential ballot.

Not waiting around to find out though, James, Sarah, and Gertrude started before dawn on the morning of June 8th for Menan, Idaho. They were off to visit daughter Jennie (as Helen was now called), her husband Charlie Ehrman and their two children, Harry, and Helen. They had an easy trip by train to Portland and left for Pocatello on the 8:25 a.m. train the next day. By nightfall, they had reached the dirty, struggling town of 4,000 inhabitants, snuggled up close to the Rocky Mountains. Early the next morning, they left Pocatello on the St. Anthony branch of the Oregon Short Line, heading for Lorenzo, Idaho. At the train station in Lorenzo, six miles from their journey's end, they were enthusiastically greeted by their son-in-law, Charlie Erhman, with a carriage awaiting. Thankfully, they all managed to fit in the carriage along with their camping gear and overnight bags. After a bumpy ride, they reached Menan and, with great joy, found Jennie's family all well and thriving. The Bushnells were so glad to be together again after a long separation.

For their July 4th celebration, Charlie proposed to take them all to visit a wonder of the world, Yellowstone National Park. It became the nation's first national park in 1872. Fortunately, the snow was nearly gone from the mountains, so they could start out on the 4th from Menan in the Erhman's carriage. But they needed help with their gear. To assist, they hired a young man with his team and wagon to haul their provisions and camping equipment. They followed the general route of the Oregon Short Line to St. Anthony, the present terminus of the railroad. St. Anthony was a fine business town situated at the Idaho Falls on the Snake River and at the end of the railroad line. There they camped on the bank of the Snake River on sandy ground so full of ant hills that they could hardly find room to stake their tents.

On the 5th of July, they had to traverse upriver and off-road nearly half a mile to find sufficient water for the animals. The next day they crossed a high range of the Sawtooth Mountains and ended up in one of the upper valleys of the North Fork of the Snake, a mostly level, wide and barren country covered with open groves of scraggly pine trees. They selected a camping spot on an immense quagmire, a swampy area that extended to the riverbank. However, this proved to be a mistake! The flies and mosquitos were so bad that they had to cover their horses with blankets and protect themselves from the biting insects with layers of clothing.

To navigate across the huge marsh the next morning, Charlie explored the way driving his heaving carriage unsteadily across the swampland and stream. They were all relieved once he made it safely across. Leaving his carriage on the far side of that marshy stream, he rode back and hitched up the other team and helped the rest of the family ride safely over.

Once all together across the marsh, they traveled slowly to face another, larger stream. This North Fork of the Snake River was about two feet deep and 400 feet wide with scarcely any bank on either side. James marveled how much easier this ford was for such a large stream. The stream bottom made of fine gravel was a much smoother surface for the wagons and horses' hooves. Riding until late at night and guided by the light of the full moon, they camped in a large, nearly level prairie with splendid grass and water everywhere. When they awoke the next morning, they found the grass frozen stiff and white with frost.

As they drove onward, they found no settlements for many miles at a stretch. About noon they reached Henry's Lake at the headwaters of the Snake, a pond-like body of water of no great depth and three or four miles across with mountains on both sides. They struck the stagecoach road on the Oregon Short Line near Monida, so-called because it is on the line between Montana and Idaho. They followed it into the mountains and crossed over a good road. In the afternoon, they crossed a branch of the Missouri and camped for the night on the banks of the Madison River. In the morning, much to their delight, they discovered that they were inside the park. Now to find the famous geysers.

They crossed another chain of the Idaho Rocky Mountains and worked their way up the Gibbon Canyon; one of the wildest, roughest and grandest scenes they'd ever beheld. Sarah marveled aloud that men had ever attempted to build a wagon road here. However, that day, the Bushnells were extremely pleased to find it to be an impressively broad, smooth road. The new road's low grade made it easy for any team to pull a heavy load up or down. They made their camp on Elk Prairie, a vast, level and grassy plain and followed the Firehole River in the morning. They camped on its banks beside a fine spring with water as cold as ice.

On July 11th, they reached the Lower Geyser Basin and began to see unique geologic phenomenas of God's creation. James and Sarah had never seen such natural wonders and were amazed and awed by the hot springs, mud pots and smelly steam vents. They found themselves unable to describe that which surrounded them on every side of their ride. They drove up to the Grand Hotel and viewed the park's largest geyser, dubbed "Old Faithful," and stopped to admire its high stream of water and steam that came at regular intervals. Leaving this awe-inspiring sight, they traveled on a mile or so and stopped for dinner along the wayside. Leaving the horses to graze, they strolled out after dinner to view some smaller geysers. After spending a few hours sightseeing, they returned to find their teams missing! The next morning, they borrowed a team from a family also camping nearby and drove to the Upper Geyser Basin. There they found their horses in a shady cluster of aspen trees. Apparently, they'd loosened their tethers and found a spot better to their liking. They camped two nights along the ridge of the Firehole River, then backtracked and took the road to the Norris Geyser Basin, another curiosity of nature. After camping at Willow Creek, they headed on to Fort Yellowstone. It didn't take much for Gertrude to talk the others into stopping and picking up a few more food supplies, including fresh tomatoes, carrots, and blackberries being sold on a cart. They supped, enjoying their fresh produce a little way farther at the base of Terrace Mountain. James raved about the flat-topped cascades of white limestone that covered many acres around them and were at least three high-terrace levels from the ground. The next day, they reached the Yellowstone River and camped above the lower falls of the same name. When they reached Yellowstone Lake, they fished all day and caught all the trout they could use. They reluctantly left the park on July 19th and took the military road south, traveling for two days along the eastern base of the beautiful Grand Teton

Mountains. On the 23rd, they spent all day, as James said, "nearer heaven than he'd ever been before." They crossed the Teton Pass at 8,428 feet high.

Two days later, they reached Menan in a heavy rainstorm. They all took baths that felt like a luxurious experience after so many days of camping out. They stayed several days with Jennie and Charlie before boarding the train at Market Lake for home.

When they reached Portland, they planned to stay a couple of nights so James could talk with the manager and inspect the freight depot and warehouse they used for his grain. Sarah convinced James that they could splurge for once, and they stayed at a new hotel on the west side of the Willamette River. The Hotel Albion was central to his business needs and to her desire to see the remnants of last year's World's Fair.

The day after they arrived, James headed off on his own toward the industrial end of town, and Sarah and Gertrude headed out to shop in the glamorous downtown Portland stores. They especially enjoyed Lippman's, where any young bride (or more mature shopper) could find all the fine things she desired to make a proper home. At age 23, Gertrude was still hoping to be a bride someday. She and her mother fingered silken fabrics and admired the variety of lovely china and crystal on display. Gertrude was especially taken with the fine linens, which were in beautiful pastels as well classic whites.

After a lovely evening in the elegant hotel, they arose the next morning to enjoy a day together exploring Portland before heading home. The three admired the new Forestry Building, still in place from the World's Fair and said to be the world's largest log cabin. They spent a few hours leisurely strolling and reading about the role of forests and timber in the building of the West. They enjoyed the beauty of the park around Guild's Lake, too. Sarah then directed them along some nearby streets to the new pink hybrid tea roses planted just for the Fair. She had read about them and wanted to see how the test roses were fairing. She was pleased to find them quite beautiful and very fragrant. As the weather was pleasant, they also enjoyed the views of Mt. St. Helens, Mt. Hood and the Willamette River from many vantage points on their walk.

The three of them travelled the rest of the way home by train, arriving back in Junction City in good health and very much strengthened by the trip. Even at nearly 80 years old, James said, "Sarah, I would very much like to do that same trip again someday!"

# CHAPTER THIRTY-SIX

ON JAMES' 80TH BIRTHDAY, some of his children planned a surprise, and he was thrilled to have unexpected morning guests. The surprise gathering included his immediate family, some other relatives and several Oregon Trail pioneer friends from 50 years before. The table that Sarah had set under the shade trees was loaded with many good things to eat. About 30 people sat down together and fully enjoyed the party. Among his guests were several pioneers of 1847 to 1851: Mr. and Mrs. Hynson Smith, aged 78 and 80; Mr. and Mrs. William A. Potter, aged 81 and 86; and Mrs. Julia Bean. James noted that "many other of their old companions had already crossed to the Eternal prairie." He said that although he was very glad to see them all, he couldn't help missing the many who were not able to attend, due to their infirmities or poor health. James proclaimed that through the mercy of his heavenly Father, he was thankful to be in fairly good health. Two of his daughters, Ollie and Jennie and their families, were not able to come either. But all the rest of his children and grandchildren were there. This was July 27, 1906.

James rarely missed a graduation ceremony, and once again he attended the Eugene Divinity School Commencement in June of 1907. At the annual Regents Meeting, he was again elected regent and lifetime president of the board. Eugene Sanderson overheard James say, "that he might as well die in the saddle as any other way." The school had proven to be highly successful and was full to capacity. The library room was overflowing with both new and donated books. Since James had been the biggest benefactor of this library, it was fitting that it was named "The Bushnell Library" that June.

The board also decided to build a new three-story stone building for classrooms and offices, the first building to be constructed on their campus. It would cost $30,000 to $35,000. James was enormously proud of the plans for the stone structure that he believed would stand for many future generations.

In July 1907, James spent another birthday quietly at home with Sarah, since their daughter Gertrude was gone most of that summer. James was in fair health again, but Sarah had her own health struggles. For the first time in many years, they opted not to go to the Turner Convention.

James and Sarah spent the rest of the summer gardening, in preparation for the Oregon State Fair. In September, they chose their best apples and other produce to compete at the fair. Together they traveled to Salem to enter their produce, attend the fair, and see his sister, Helen, who'd moved to Salem. After a good visit and catching up on the family events, they all attended the new Salem Christian Church together on Sunday. James and Sarah hurried back home to Junction City that same night because they were expecting a visit from Gertrude the very next day.

Gertrude had spent part of her summer in Ashland with Ollie. The two sisters enjoyed each other, and Gertrude helped with the children who were all home on summer vacation. Then, Gertrude had gone on to Seattle and attended the Christian Endeavor Convention. Upon arriving home from all this, she filled her parents' ears with all she had seen and done. She especially extolled the bold plans the Christian Endeavor group had for the Pacific Northwest region. Appreciating his daughter's enthusiasm for spiritual things, James listened and encouraged her.

When the Bushnells attended the Spring commencement in 1908, change was afoot. The Regents had voted to change the school's name to "Eugene Bible University." This year out of the six graduates, four of them were ordained for the ministry. James and Sarah relished the chance to inspect the foundation of the new stone building that lay 60 by 80 feet. They were impressed that the Regents planned to have this building ready for the coming fall term.

**The first graduating class**

The school's stone building that James was so proud of

Later that same month, James, Sarah, and Gertrude left for the yearly Turner Camp Meeting. Upon arrival, they fixed up their cabin and settled in, then visited old friends before the service started at 8:00 p.m. It was a grand reunion since James and Sarah had missed the previous year. They were also eager to hear the main speaker, President E. V. Zollars of Oklahoma University, considered one of the best teachers in the nation. He gave a fine address. During the two weeks of meetings, the Bushnells met people from different quarters of the Earth, such as the Dyes, missionaries from Bolengie, others from Central Africa, and the Stephens from New Zealand. The states of California, Washington, Idaho, Ohio, and Kansas were all represented in Turner, as well. James was delighted to greet many of his old friends, but he told Sarah that he missed a great many more who had already passed on. He was proud to say, though, that his younger friends included the alumni of the Eugene Divinity School, now some of the best preachers of the day.

He commented to Sarah that night, "I can't make friends as easily as I once did, but I do think just as much of them once they are made." She responded, "Oh, applesauce! I've never seen another man with as many friends as you have, James. Yes, you've lost some due to death, but you know you can't go down a street in Junction City or around Eugene without finding someone to chat with."

She clasped his hand and continued, "I think you're just in a sentimental mood back here at the camp where so many of your dear friendships were formed." He squeezed her hand and smiled softly. "I suppose you may be right."

As usual, the camp ran through the Fourth of July. For the afternoon program, the Young People's Christian Endeavor led the day and filled the camp's amphitheater seats. Then, that night, Brother Stephens gave a splendid patriotic address. The three Bushnells left the camp on July 6th and arrived home tired but inspired.

A quiet day with family was all James wanted for his 82nd birthday. Sarah and Gertrude noted that he did not act very strong that summer. Perhaps partly, they thought, because the summer was so hot.

During the 95-degree heat, James got a call from Dean Sanderson on August 3rd, inviting him to come and look over the new building and some changes that had been made at the Bible University. Despite the sweltering temperatures, James and Sarah boarded the early train and rode into Eugene. They were pleased to see the progress on the new building's white stone exterior and the near completion of the slate roof. All the construction seemed to be on schedule. The founders still hoped to have it ready for occupancy by the start of school on September 22.

And as hoped, it opened then with much fanfare! Sarah was especially delighted that this new building now housed The Bushnell Library, too.

# CHAPTER THIRTY-SEVEN

## *James starts another new project*

THE HEAT CONTINUED IN the 90–95-degree range daily for three weeks and there was little rain for over two months. Confined indoors, mostly due to the heat, James began dreaming up another way to make their life better. He had recently read in the *Oregon Statesman* that some residences were putting in indoor plumbing. He brought up the idea to Sarah one evening.

"I realize that it's getting harder and harder for me to get to the out-house. And I'm worried I'll burden you with my chamber pot duties as I keep getting older. So, I think it's time I build us our own indoor toilet and bathroom. I've been reading about them and am ready to send for the toilet and the instructions from this here company recommended in the newspaper."

Sarah stopped her knitting and faced him. Looking him straight in the eye, she declared, "James, you're 82 years old! Why would you want to start such a big project like that now?'

He grinned back at her and simply said, "I have the building bug again. And for your information, this one will be easier than the other projects I've been considering lately." And he quickly kept talking. "The first thing I need to do is dig a hole big enough for the septic tank. I know that will mess up our lawn on the east side for a bit, but eventually the grass will grow back again to nicely cover it all. Digging will be simple and easy enough for me to start on my own. As soon as the weather cools off, that is. I think that's maybe in a few more weeks. In the meantime, I can be measuring and sharpening my shovels." He finally paused.

Sarah sighed. "I am not saying that I wouldn't appreciate indoor plumbing. It's a wonderful idea, as we've discussed before. I just worry that you're too old to manage all that work by yourself. I would like to live out a few more years — together, you know. Could you at least get Royal or William to help you with the digging?"

"Well, maybe Royal or a neighbor, but William will be too busy with the harvest," he replied. "For now, I'll just get to measuring for placing the cesspool at the right distance from the house. That will take hardly any effort and give me something interesting to do. Then when I'm ready for it, I'll see if Royal can give me a hand with the digging."

He looked at her with a reassuring smile and nod. She just barely smiled back at him.

When September arrived, Sarah was so thankful that Royal could help James. The two men started sharpening the tools and measuring out the dimensions in the Bushnells' yard. The day they began digging, several neighborhood boys stopped by. They were eager to watch the Bushnells' digging and the hole grow bigger. Some even wanted to help dig, which James encouraged. He joked with Sarah that he was glad he hadn't hired any help, since he had all the free labor he needed from these neighborhood boys. By and by, the huge hole was dug and then they lined it with fine gravel along the bottom. All these procedures became quite the neighborhood spectacle for youth and adults alike.

Sarah couldn't stop James from ripping down half of their kitchen and dining room wall all by himself, though. The 82-year-old seemed to thoroughly enjoy the demolition job. Their new bathroom was to be off the kitchen on the east side of their home. James planned for a new, enclosed bathroom with two doors, one off the kitchen and one leading to their bedroom. The heavy water tank would eventually be mounted several feet above the toilet bowl. That wall would require reinforcement, and James undertook to complete that task himself, also.

Then the indoor measuring began. James measured the distance from where the toilet bowl would sit on the floor to the water tank above it at least three times. Sarah helped with that. Then, they measured several times for the pipe to go through the hole through the wall to the outdoors. The last step was measuring down the wall and over to their underground system.

James was gleeful when he brought the new copper plumbing piping home from Eugene. He pranced around the house as he showed it off to Sarah. Then, next Royal helped him measure and remeasure the tubing before James did the cutting with his sharp saw. Sarah hated that loud grinding noise and stayed inside with the windows closed while this part happened. With these steps completed, they seemed ready for their new bathroom fixtures, and for those to arrive they now to just had to wait. Happily, their wait was but two days.

When the Oregon-California train brought their porcelain toilet bowl and matching tank into town, the Allen boy himself carefully wheeled the crates over to their house on the railroad cart. This personal delivery brought many of the adult neighbors out to watch, too. Once it was in the Bushnell's yard, the shiny white pieces were carefully unloaded and gently placed in the grass. Now, even Sarah took pleasure in the ruckus their new bathroom was causing. Amused by all the interest, she began making plans for some small tea parties so she could introduce the new plumbing to the neighborhood women and the town. For now, though, she and James needed to decide where to store their porcelain beauties.

With the decision made, James asked the Allen boy to help him carry them up the steps and onto the porch. When both pieces were set, James tipped the boy and waved goodbye to the crowd. He announced to the gathered neighbors that he would start in the morning fitting the piping and with that said the two Bushnells grasped hands, turned, and walked inside.

The next morning James was up early and whistling while he shaved. Once again, Sarah marveled at his energy. She rose much more slowly but was determined to fix him a good breakfast: eggs and bacon with leftover biscuits. She waited until after he'd eaten before inquiring about the process of moving the toilet pieces from the porch to the bathroom. James told her he was going to take Ray Roberts up on his offer and ask him to come help with the lifting. He was off to fetch the neighbor before she'd even finished her coffee. James and Ray stopped on the Bushnells' porch to first discuss the lifting and carrying of the water tank inside to the new bathroom. Carefully the two men carried the load and turning it sideways to fit inside the front hallway and then through Sarah's kitchen. Ray politely begged her pardon.

"Nonsense," she replied. "You're a welcome help, Ray."

After the men set the tank down along the wall, James climbed up his ladder and checked once more to be sure the pipe was secure in the wall. Securing that, he and Ray heaved the tank onto the ladder's top and studied the pipe's hole. Then, Rory appeared. James' premade shelf was already on the wall. The three men moved the tank over onto the shelf, and then all three stood back with relief to admire their work. "Now, to see if the pipes are going to fit together," James declared. He guided the tank closer to the wall pipe until it met the other pipe. He was able to wrench them together. Now, their audience had grown to include Sarah and Mrs. Roberts, too, and they all cheered and applauded this feat.

Connecting the tank to the toilet bowl was the next big step, and it also went smoothly. It took some jerry-rigging to get the bowl into the proper place and the pipe adjusted in length, but "not bad for half a day's work," James bragged when he stood back and looked it all over. Then he asked

Sarah to hand him the brass chain with the smooth wooden handle. He easily got that fastened and hanging from the tank above. Sarah said cheerfully, "It all looks so nice, except for the shavings and mess on the floor. But I can clean that up soon enough."

"It is very impressive, but will it really work?" she wondered much more quietly.

As if hearing her last thought, James said, "Now, to see if it's going to work! I need to go out to the pumphouse and start the water flowing again," and he departed through the new door into the kitchen. The others stayed in the bathroom still admiring this shiny, white, amazing invention that was waiting to be proven.

Once James returned, he told them all to listen for the sound of the water filling the tank on the wall. Mrs. Roberts and Sarah both gasped when they heard water filling the pipes and tank. "It's like music to my ears" sighed Sarah. The women clapped at such a pleasing noise!

"I agree it is a lovely sound," Ray said, and all the rest just grinned and slapped James on the back.

In one more minute, James gave Sarah the honor of pulling the new chain. Holding her breath, she pulled down hard. Sure enough! Water flowed down into the bowl and ran out the bottom pipe.

Now they all really celebrated, applauding loudly and with shouts this time! Royal danced a jig around Sarah and James. He declared, "People would pay you just to watch this, Grandpa! You could get some money out of your investment here."

James grinned back saying, "I'd rather just let my family and guests use it and enjoy it with us. But thanks for the idea in case I'm ever in need of some quick cash."

# CHAPTER THIRTY-EIGHT

IN DECEMBER, JAMES WAS still finishing the improvements to their bathroom when he sprained his ankle stepping off the ladder. He was laid up for some time watching it rain and snow out the windows. He watched the Willamette flood again and run wild through the streets of the town. Fortunately, the water did no particular damage this time.

That winter was bitterly cold, and at 84 years old, James was feeling worn and weary. One blustery afternoon, Sarah was listening to James reading his Bible aloud near the kitchen fire. She had just taken a break from chopping dried fruits for her pies, then brewed them some tea and sat. James stopped and looked up as she sat down in her rocking chair.

"Sarah, I just cannot take in all my blessings. I have the special treasures of loving children and friends, and all this world's goods. In fact, I was just thinking that we have more goods than we can use. I would like to put more of our money into something of definite eternal value. Something that will last long after we do."

"James dear, your investment in the lives of our children will last for many generations. Your investment in the Junction City community should last for many decades at least. And the time and money you've put into the Bible University certainly counts for eternity. And those are just the first things that come quickly to my mind. I am sure I could list more with some additional thought."

"Yes, I hear what you're saying, Sarah," and he nodded with a half-smile. "However, I think there is still more I can do before I pass from this Earth."

Sarah reached over and patted his hand. "We'll just pray about that, then. God will show us if there is more He'd like us to do. And we will do it together. Keep praying over it, James."

Within the month, it was Sarah who was divinely inspired. She and James had attended the Commencement Ceremony for the Eugene Bible University and proudly watched six more men be ordained. However, James had almost burst with pride as he introduced the main speaker of the day, O. S. C. Humbert. Humbert had been their very first graduate back in 1899!

At the reception afterward in the library, Sarah and Prudence Sanderson got to visit alone, without their husbands around. As usual, it didn't take long for them to go from inquiring about each other's health to the inevitable next question, which always was "Does your husband have any new ideas for the school?" Both women had found it was almost inevitable that one husband or the other would have a new proposal.

"Well," Prudence lowered her voice, "and this is strictly in confidence for you and James only. My Eugene is fancying to gather up more old, historical Bibles. He would love to get a good collection built and then house them in the college's library." She shook her head, "I don't think he can ever quit scheming. In fact, ever since I've known him, Sarah, one of his passions has been looking for old Bibles. He just loves to hunt for them, and he even reads them, too. So, his latest idea is all a great fantasy for sure, because neither the school nor we have that kind of money. It would cost him quite a lot to go back to Europe and find the kind of antique Bibles he's talking about. So, as I've learned, I just let him talk and try not to discourage him, especially after some of his dreams have actually come true—-like this school for example! If his ideas are from God, then God will take care of it all."

"My, what an intriguing hobby, and what a vision," declared Sarah in response. "I am impressed your Eugene isn't completely overwhelmed with all his responsibilities at the college and within the churches. I suppose nothing will stop our husbands from new adventures, though; even old age cannot, in James' instance. He just told me last week that he still wants his life to count for something good; more than he's already done. So, there he goes, still dreaming at age 84."

Prudence reached over and patted Sarah's gloved hand. "That is very nice for me to hear. An elder who isn't sitting back in his rocker and hasn't given up trying to serve others. Isn't that what we really want in a husband, Sarah? A man still seeking to please God all of his days here on Earth?"

Sarah squeezed the hand over hers and smiled in return. "You're exactly right, dear. It makes me quite proud of him. Now and then, I do start to worry about his health, though. The recent winters haven't been easy for him."

"Well, you are both often in our prayers. And we sure need your support in carrying out so much of Eugene's work and vision here. It is a great blessing to both of us to have you in our lives. Please pass that onto James for me, won't you?"

The two women were then interrupted by loud applause all over the Reception Room for the entering graduates. Their conversation was over for the day, as all the applause was followed by toasts and short speeches. Then, others came to mingle and visit with these two revered women.

After church two days later, Sarah broached the subject with her husband "I can't get this idea out of my head, James. Every time I pick up my Bible, it comes back to me. Even when I see you pick up your old Bible, it triggers this idea. This might be important for you to know. Prudence told me about a new idea of Eugene's. Or at least the part about involving the school, is a new idea. She said that he loves looking for, and discovering, old Bibles. The older the better. Did you already know that?"

James nodded and replied, "It does not come as a surprise. He's spoken about seeing and collecting fascinating old Bibles back at Yale. Also, I know he wants to author a book about the English Bible."

"Well, according to Prudence, he is now dreaming about collecting incredibly old Bibles, like ancient historical ones. He envisions going back to Europe to find and buy the oldest ones he can. But he doesn't have the funds for such a trip or the means for purchasing once he gets there. Ever since I heard this, I've been wondering if it would be a good use of our money— towards something that lasts eternally? You know, as you said a few days back?"

"What's the part where the school gets involved?" James asked.

"Oh, yes, that. Well, he thinks this European collection should be housed in the library, so that our students and faculty would benefit from it there."

James quickly picked up the vision. "Not only students and faculty. I think it should be open to the public, too. People will be stirred by such a treasure and be reminded that many people risked or gave up their lives to bring us the Bible, especially one in our own language. Think of the educational value and the history we could display! It would demonstrate the longevity of God's Word and its continued popularity throughout the ages, even into our world today. Yes, this would be a very worthy endeavor, Sarah, adding greatly to our ministry in Eugene and all the community around. People would be drawn to it from all over the region and it would help promote the school as well."

They were both quiet for a moment, pondering all he'd just said.

James broke the silence first. "We need to pray about this, Sarah, but I think it is quite exciting!"

Within six months, Dean Sanderson was off on a sabbatical to study on the East Coast and then on to Oxford, England. He proposed to use the year to better prepare himself with more intensive study for his teaching.

With a generous gift of $1,000 from the Bushnells, he also planned using his spare time perusing old bookshops for the oldest and rarest Bibles he could find. His proposal met with unanimous approval: to take time off from his teaching for professional studies and to search out the Bibles he desired. So, Sanderson spent his days away from Oregon with some higher-level studies and concentrated course work. Even with all his schoolwork, Sanderson still managed to visit six countries and purchase close to 120 old Bibles and religious books in his spare time.

Upon returning home, Eugene privately told James that this new Bible collection would be named in honor of the Bushnells and placed in the school's library. With great gratitude, James insisted that it would be only in Sarah's name, though. He explained that God had inspired Sarah with this worthwhile cause, and he'd just jumped on board. As usual, nobody argued very long with James Bushnell. Consequently, the Sarah E. Bushnell Bible and Rare Book Collection was created.

# CHAPTER THIRTY-NINE

ON MAY 23, 1911, just one year before he died, James enjoyed another special time at the Divinity School's alumni banquet in the Eugene Christian Church. There were about 40 alumni attending and James had helped ordain all of them as preachers! He took his place as President of the Board, just as he had for 15 years ever since the opening day of the school. Because Dean Sanderson was still recovering from his sabbatical in England, James delivered the Annual Address. He extolled the growth of the school from its beginning in a rented room with six students and no property, to the current attendance of 157 students, with four good buildings, and assets of over $150,000. Also, he added that the school's current alumni represented preachers in every state on the Pacific coast.

No one was surprised that James was reelected to continue in his position for three more years. He admitted to Sarah that he "did not expect to fill it out, but God alone knows. If it is His will that I should tarry here three years longer, I shall be glad. If not, I shall be the same." The Regents' meeting was held around the large table in the Bushnell Library, a fine spacious room in the stone building. The library contained 3,000 to 4,000 volumes; the majority personally donated by James himself.

In fact, his last recorded words before his death at age 85, were about his contributions. "The library is supposed to keep in memory the name of J.A. Bushnell when he is dead and otherwise forgotten—it is well. I have never been ashamed of my record. It will matter little to me if my name is only in the Lamb's Book of Life, but for my children's sake may they remember with gratitude." He also noted his appreciation for his loving relationship with Sarah in their marriage of 36 years.

This remarkable man died quietly at home with his family in April of 1912.

At his funeral, one of his longtime friends from the Christian Church and Divinity School, said "James Bushnell had more ideas and energy in his life than three other men put together."

His brother Corydon reminisced about plowing the virgin soil in the Grand Prairie and setting up their lean-tos there together. Cory went on to describe James' many endeavors, from "starting a homestead farm, to teaching school in a smoky cabin, to building granaries and a bank, running an opera house, and founding a Divinity School. That's my brother. That man could do anything he put his mind to."

James Bushnell, who had very few years of formal education himself, founded a college that still thrives 127 years later. Additionally, he left his lasting imprint on the community he loved that prospered in great part because of his leadership, Christian resolve, and abundant service to many organizations, institutions, and many individuals.

**James, Sarah and Gertrude Bushnell**

# CHAPTER FORTY

## *Life Goes on for Sarah*

SARAH HAD BEEN WIDOWED now for about three years and was home, quietly knitting by her fire. She jumped when Gertrude rushed inside, breathless with shocking news. Their hotel was on fire! Gertrude had rushed over as soon as she'd heard the news from Henry. He'd been downtown and had seen the buildings burning himself. The clanging of the fire bell interrupted Gertrude as she was telling Sarah; she had gotten there that fast. Within a few minutes more, Nettie arrived. She reported that William and their boys had dropped her off so she could be with Sarah while they hurried off to help the fire fighters. Absorbing the news slowly, Sarah walked to the fireplace and began praying aloud. Her daughters noticed that her prayers were mostly for the safety of everyone in the hotel and for the men trying to save the building—rather than for the building itself. Nettie and Gertrude listened and murmured agreements along with Sarah in her prayers. Soon, young Francis knocked loudly on their door and hollered that the fire was spreading and now covered about half the block. He added that the fire department was hard at work trying to control it, but it looked very discouraging.

Sarah silently walked to the hallway coat hook, grabbed her coat and put it on. Firmly but sadly, she said, "I need you to walk me over there, Francis. I want to see this for myself. Those buildings are like family to me. Your grandfather and I put our hearts and souls into them."

Francis looked at his mother, who nodded and reached for her coat, too. The four of them walked as swiftly as Sarah was able, over to Front Street, with Francis holding his grandmother's arm as they walked. They stopped within a block of the fire and watched as the brick hotel and stores crumbled in the soaring flames. They were soon forced to watch their ballroom and then the Opera House engulfed in the inferno. Sarah sighed and wiped tears while holding onto Gertrude for support. She watched long enough to know that the whole city block was likely to burn. The city's cultural enterprises, which had brought such pleasure to so many, including their family, were now aflame and bursting with small explosions here and there. It was a personal disaster for the Bushnells.

It was also a community disaster. After 23 years of providing civic enrichment and entertainment in Junction City, the Bushnell's hotel and opera house were destroyed by a small spark—one that changed community life forever. (This extensive fire ended up changing the growth patterns of the town, too. The town's commercial center began shifting to the west and away from the river and lowlands that annually flooded.)

"I've seen enough now," Sarah stated simply after 30 minutes of standing and staring at the burning buildings. "Please take me home."

The three women turned for home and Francis went over to talk to his brothers. Wanting to help in any way he could, he walked around the busy scene a bit looking for an opportunity to assist. Then, he resigned himself to just standing there with Clarence, both silently watching and feeling totally helpless.

Over the next couple of days, the adult Bushnell children came together in Junction City to help their mother through her shock and with all the cleanup. It was a busy time for Nettie, Glenn, Henry, and Gertrude, who all lived close by. Ollie came up from Ashland. However, they'd convinced Jennie over the telephone that she needn't come from Idaho. The five Bushnells all took their turns picking through the mess of wet ashes and scorched bricks, hoping to salvage some things of use or of value. Unfortunately, they found very little salvageable.

Glenn and Henry worked with the insurance company and processed the family's financial loss. Thankfully, they'd kept their block of buildings maintained up to the city code and the insurance policies were all current and paid. The sons were able to comfort their mother with that much news, at least.

Sarah was now 69 years old, with only a recent decline in her health. Her children noticed after the big fire that she grieved mostly about the emotional and personal losses, not finances. She expressed this to Gertrude saying it wasn't the loss of income that bothered her as much as the loss of the dreams that she and James had built together. She had no heart or will to discuss any possibility of rebuilding the ballroom, opera house, or even the hotel. Without Sarah's motivation or interest, and with some concern for their mother's health, the Bushnell children all decided there was no good reason to rebuild these establishments. None of them envisioned any of those businesses in their own futures. Hence, James and Sarah's businesses closed, all except the Farmers and Merchant Bank. Most of their parents' civic dreams were gone.

Sarah lived a few years in town alone, but eventually moved in with her daughter Gertrude and son-in-law Robert Movins. When Sarah died on January 29, 1916, she was buried alongside James and 15 other Bushnells in the Luper Cemetery, south of Junction City. Her burial was near the early Clear Lake where James had helped start a church. It is now the present-day Irving area northwest of Eugene.

## BUSHNELL UNIVERSITY
## SEPTEMBER 30, 2021

Pushing her 96-year-old mother in a wheelchair, Kathy led the way across the green lawn outlined by striking oranges, yellows, and reds in the bordering trees. "Isn't it a beautiful day in the Northwest?" she murmured loud enough for her mother to hear. They were headed to the University auditorium for the evening's program. Following them were her siblings Dan and LuAnn, her daughter Angela, and her granddaughters, Joya and Faith. They had already taken several family pictures at the old stone building across the street and at the brick library beyond that.

Faith bounced up from behind to get near her grandmother, "Grammy, I see another sign that says Bushnell. I've counted five now!"

"Oh good. I see it too now, Faith. How about you, Joya? Do you see it?" Kathy stopped pushing and turned to her little granddaughters. They had been counting how many times they saw the name "Bushnell" on the university campus.

Two of the families had made the trip to Eugene from their homes in Vancouver and it had taken them over two hours on the freeway to get here. Faith knew that Grammy's friend, Ms. Jenn, had wanted them all to come and she knew that Grammy really, really had wanted them all to be here together. This old school had something to do with their family and the name Bushnell. Still wondering about that, Faith ran back to her mom and asked quietly so Grammy wouldn't hear her, "Mom, what does this school have to do with our family again?"

Angela smiled and replied softly, "Remember your great-grandfather, the one we always just called 'Great?' She paused and Faith nodded in acknowledgement. "Well, when he was a baby and up until your age and to the age of 13, his grandmother lived with him in that old farmhouse in Junction

City. The one where Uncle Josh lives now. Do you remember that old yellow house?"

"Well, before she got married to a Pitney, his grandmother's name was Lucy Jennette Bushnell. She lived with your 'Great' and his family when he was a boy in that old yellow house. It was Lucy's father that helped build and start this school. He started it to instruct young men and women about the Bible so they could be ministers and teachers in the churches."

Apparently, Grammy had been listening to them anyway, because now she said to Faith, "Way back then, they called it Eugene Divinity School. When I was growing up it was called Northwest Christian College. Then it changed to 'Northwest Christian University' as it got larger. And just last year, they changed its name again. You know what the new name is, right, Faith and Joya?"

Younger Joya, wanting to beat her sister, shouted "Bushnell University!" first.

"Yes, and that's why we see all these new signs with the Bushnell name on them. Although, it has been over a year since the school began using the new name. They weren't able to celebrate it until now and I bet you know why!"

"COVID," both girls said in unison, dragging out the word like the bad memory it was.

"So here we are a year later, finally ready to help celebrate this big event with all these university folks."

The staff of the newly renamed Bushnell University had invited them all to attend the Founders' Day Celebration on the school's 126th anniversary. All but Kathy's mom were descendants of its first founder and president, her great-great grandfather James A. Bushnell. Kathy was happy and proud to be here with the four generations of Bushnell-Pitneys present. As they walked in and were seated, Kathy put her hand on her mom's and said quietly, "If only Dad was here to see this. He would have been so proud."

"Stop that now, before you make me cry," her mother said. And with that, they both turned to the front and settled into the welcoming words of the university president.

# *Epilogue*

## NETTIE'S TRUNK
## SEPTEMBER 1872

SHE FELT SAD, ANXIOUS, and excited all at the same time! The day had finally arrived to pack the wooden trunk her mother had given her years ago upon her eighth-grade graduation. Nettie especially loved the trunk now, four years after her mother had died. Slowly and lovingly, she ran her hand over the smooth brown wood and shiny metal trim. Then, with the same hand, she wiped the runaway tear from her cheek. But she straightened her shoulders, determined only to think about the future right now. She had important packing to accomplish.

Today the trunk seemed too small to contain all the personal belongings she wanted it to hold. She'd been wondering for weeks just what to pack and what to leave at home. Looking at the piles laying out around her on the bed, she was still wondering. Never having been away from home for more than two nights, Nettie tried to predict what the next two-and-a-half months held for her. Also, she knew she'd be sharing a large bedroom with two other girls, and personal space would be limited. Monmouth Christian College students boarded in local homes, and she was about to become one of the six boarders in the home of her favorite Aunt Helen and Uncle George.

For as long as Nettie could remember, she'd been expecting to get a college education. Her older brother, Charles, had gone to Monmouth before her. Her parents were encouraging it. Yet, she only knew of one other girl planning to go on past the local grammar and high schools in Junction City. That girlfriend was going to the University of Oregon in Eugene, while she was headed to Monmouth. About three years ago, her dear Aunt Helen and Uncle Edward had moved to Monmouth just to support the school. Their church had envisioned a supportive Christian community built all around the college and its students. Her aunt and uncle had personally adopted that vision. Nettie and her family had visited them in Monmouth, and she was excited to move to a bigger town!

However, now the inevitable was pressing upon her. She re-focused on her packing job by looking all around her room. She was fairly certain that she would need at least one carpet bag in addition to her trunk. She grabbed her two pairs of shoes and her pair of winter boots first and pushed them down into the bottom of the trunk. Those alone filled almost half the trunk. She realized she could get some undergarments and stockings tucked inside the shoes and boots. After doing that, she smiled at her own cleverness. Next, she decided to pack her Bible and four notebooks. They all fit nicely into the upper shelf hinged inside the trunk's lid. She carefully wrapped her framed family picture from Father and Sarah's wedding day in a wool scarf. It also fit in that top lid compartment. That was easy enough.

She looked at her wool coat and long dresses and wondered again how she'd get such bulky items packed. The best idea seemed to be to wear her coat or simply carry it, even though it was still a pleasant fall. With that decision made, she rolled her three dresses and got two packed in well enough. She put the other one inside her carpet bag. In the trunk there was still room for one towel in the top alongside her Bible and notebooks. That was it for the top. Then, she happily wrapped her few jewelry pieces inside two washrags and folded them to fit in the trunk shelf compartments. This lift-off shelf covered the top of the open trunk. She put a bar of soap, comb, hairbrush, one set of black leather gloves, three hankies, and a powder compact given to her by Sarah in the smaller compartments. She dropped two ink pens, a tightly screwed bottle of ink, and a handful of lead pencils into the lid's shelf. Everything seemed to fit well and was sensibly packed. She was feeling quite satisfied until she looked around her room. Her eyes lit on her bedding and popped wide open. She sighed. Removing her third dress from the carpet bag, she folded the quilt and pushed it down as hard as she could to the bottom of the empty bag. Two cotton sheets filled the rest of the bag with a pillowcase laid on top. Her carpetbag was now really a "bedding bag," she mused. At least it all fit!

Lifting the compartment shelf out of her trunk again, she stuffed her third dress inside. She could get it all in if she pushed the shelf back down firmly. Then she carefully shut the trunk lid and gingerly sat upon it. Awkwardly between her skirt and legs, she managed to lock it securely. She'd gotten everything she wanted in it and was content with the one extra bag. Anything else that she might remember later would have to go in a second bag.

With sweet memories, she looked around her room. She knew that soon after she was gone, her father and Sarah planned to build another house and move into town. This room wouldn't be here anymore, and this house wouldn't be home when she came back in December. She would miss all the good family times they'd had here, but she had plenty of heartbreaking memories here, too. She'd helped nurse her ailing mother while assisting her father run the household. Then, she'd watched her mother die, and her father and siblings grieve in this house. Less than six years later, her closest sibling—her older brother Charles— came home to die here, too. Charles had been a kind brother and understood her better than anyone else. She'd really missed him the two years he moved away to college. He didn't make it into his third year of college due to his fragile health. He came home for Christmas, and they all were forced to watch him get weaker and weaker. Nettie had spent several months helping nurse Charles and helping Sarah run the household. It was still painful, thinking about watching her dear brother die. He was gone by early February.

She remembered how she, 12-year-old Helen, and Papa grieved in a way that only the three of them shared, losing their big brother and eldest son. This sorrow drew them together and they'd sit in the evenings by the fire in comforting silence. Her stepmother, Sarah, had also lost many of her dearest loved ones, and had been widowed twice as a young bride. She understood their pain and let them grieve together, father and daughters. Nettie knew that Sarah, too, had loved Charles.

Shaking her head clear of these sad memories, Nettie again turned her mind from the past to the future ahead of her. She was going to college and moving to Monmouth this very day! She believed good things were to come and she looked forward to sweet Aunt Helen's comfort and encouragement.

## NETTIE'S TRUNK—KATHLEEN PITNEY BOX SEPTEMBER 1969

When I packed the trunk my grandfather, Clarence Pitney, grandson of James Bushnell, passed down to my parents, I felt a strong connection to Nettie, and my Bushnell relatives over 100 years ago. Grandpa's mother, Lucy Jennette Bushnell Pitney, took this very same, small wooden trunk when she left for college back in 1872. I was also leaving home to begin my freshman year at Oregon State University in Corvallis, only twenty miles from the Monmouth College where Nettie went. I was proud to be taking a family heirloom with me on my journey.

During the summer before my college experience, my mother wanted my help refinishing the old family trunk before sending us both off to school. She showed me how to strip the dark ancient varnish off the trunk and we worked together to change the color. The old wood soon turned into a light green stain with gold antiquing. The antiquing was a popular finishing treatment in the 1960's. Inside the trunk, the original wood was rough and uneven. We remedied that by covering it with small floraled contact-paper in an orange and white pattern.

My trunk was soon packed with many personal items, like the long, orange scarf with long, black fringe knitted by my Aunt Gerry; twin bed sheets; my handmade black-and-white flowered quilt that I'd tied with knotted orange yarn; and a pillow. I was adopting the college colors orange and black into my dormitory life. All these almost filled the trunk. On top of that, I laid the shallow wooden shelf where I placed my Bible, a paperback dictionary and thesaurus, knitted gloves and matching hat. In the upper compartment went new spiral notebooks and a framed picture of my family. Like Nettie, I would soon share a room with one to three new roommates each term over the next four years.

Eventually, the trunk went with me from the dorm to the sorority house, and later to my first job in Southern California. Then, the trunk and I both returned to Oregon a year later, moving into my first home as a newlywed. That first home was older than the state of Oregon, and the trunk fit perfectly in the old white farmhouse. In all, it would accompany me on our moves to four other homes, all in Oregon and Washington.

Currently, in the year 2022, Nettie's trunk is now settled with me in house number five in Vancouver, Washington, the town where I've lived for the past 40 years. Even as I write this today, I can see the pale green trunk on my upstairs' floor landing.

Above the trunk, I proudly display my grandmother's gold shadow box, holding several antique photographs of various ancestors. The largest photo is of my great-great grandfather James Bushnell. I am descended from pioneer stock on both sides of my family. From its outside, the trunk still looks lovely with the antique gold finish on its pale green wood. Inside though, it shows its age of at least 146 years. The original leather hinge holding the upper shelf needs repairing. In many places the contact paper is peeling away from the original rough wood. Today, and through all those 50 years with me, the contents are still mostly personal mementos from my Oregon State University days. I just took out the orange and black knit scarf a few years back and passed it on to my nephew, when he attended Oregon State.

I believe I have treasured the old wooden trunk with its metal trim almost as much as Nettie did, as we both left our parents' homes and headed toward futures that God only knew. Looking back on our lives, great-grandmother and great-granddaughter, it turned out that we were both blessed to overflowing.

# *Acknowledgments*

I HAVE MANY, MANY people to thank, starting with my new friends at the now Bushnell University. (When I started my research, it was named Northwest Christian University.) I was greeted with a warm welcome by Dr. Womack, his assistant Jennifer Box, and then librarian Steve Silver, among others. Since then, I've had many tours of the campus but Steve's tour of the Sarah Bushnell Rare Bible and Book Collection for my extended family will never be forgotten. Also, his published literary piece on Eugene Sanderson's book-buying trip to Europe and complete account of the collection was very helpful and interesting.

Jennifer Box has been a constant help and encouragement. And no, even though we have the same last name we aren't related and had never met before! Her love of the school's history and all the area's local history inspires me every time we get together. She has given me photos and documents our family had never seen. She is never too busy for me, and I know she is a very busy person.

Bill DiMarco, the tireless leader of the Junction City Historical Society, is a fount of wisdom. He has guided me, supplied me with answers, and has been a big overall encouragement. He has a vast knowledge of all things regarding Junction City history and promptly replied to my many questions.

Alice Pitney Norris is my dear cousin, the absolutely best family historian, and Oregon historian extraordinaire. She spent numerous days and countless hours editing and doing her own research for this endeavor. And she acted like she was enjoying it! Having been an English teacher and is also an avid historian, she was the perfect resource for me. She is the keeper of generations worth of our family documents and memories. She knows her stuff!

When I got Alice's help, I was doubly blessed with her husband's historical knowledge and resources. Mike Norris contributed valuable insights and details pertinent to the era I was covering.

I met a new friend towards the end of my writing that assisted me, too. Carol Cure offered enthusiastic support, more editing, and her own family history. Editing the manuscript, she soon discovered that her family is the very Henderson Murphy family that James and Sarah go to visit in eastern Washington. What a small world!

Lane County Historical Society showed me helpful documents that I could copy or purchase. I did both. They had documents that I hadn't seen, and I now love owning. Thank you for being there for researchers like me.

My 97-year-old mother, Barbara McFadden Pitney, helped me with some specific memories, answered my questions, and was a continual encouragement. Living together as I tackled this project, she had to listen more to me than anyone else. I know she is glad it's all done.